RipHer

Lee Leslie

RIPHER

Printed in the United States of
America
Sherrel Lee
P O Box 865073
Plano, TX 75086-5073
Email: sherrellee.valens@gmail.com
Twitter: @gryphoenix

Cover: Depositphotos.com, *Bloody
Wall* © Stephanie Frey #5390850All
rights reserved

First Edition

ACKNOWLEDGEMENTS

Thank you to all those who have worked with me over the years to help the publication of this work become reality. To my family who has had to sit back and give me the time and space to work, my critique partners Diane and Angela who have worked to keep me on target and don't allow me to drift off into other tales when I am trying to work on one at a time. To the distributors of new book formats that make it possible for the story to be told. And I want to say a special thank you to the readers who have taken a chance on a new author and a new twist to the story.

FACT: Between April and December 1888 five prostitutes were murdered Mary Ann Nichols, Annie Chapman, Elizabeth Stride, Catherine "Kate" Eddowes and Mary Jane Kelly.

FACT: Four of the five women were known to have lived on Dorset Street which was called the most dangerous street in London.

FACT: Mary Jane Kelly was "turned out" to become a prostitute by her cousin in Ireland.

FACT: Hundreds of theories abound about who the killer was, but there has never been a final resolution to the crimes.

It is time to learn the truth.

Contents

PROLOGUE
February, 1888

The carriage wheels creaked as they bumped along the dark rutted path. Fog blanketed the land and muffled the sound of the horses' hooves. She peered at a small halo of light that barely penetrated the mist in the distance as the horses slowed to a stop. Lady Rowena Radcliffe pulled her cloak tight and prepared herself for what was to come.

In the distance, men huddled together in the center of a field. An amber pool of light was too weak to show the object of their attention. She recognized the acrid and unmistakable scent of death before she looked upon the pale figure sprawled in the weeds.

A constable guarded the path, and spat on the ground as she approached. Though it was too dark to see, she knew disapproval was etched across his face.

Relieved he could not see the flush of indignation his actions caused, she pressed on. Tonight was the wrong time to let these men know how their prejudices affected her.

"Lady Radcliffe, I was surprised to find you were already in the area."

"Inspector Layne," she stopped as he approached. "Please refer me as Doctor Radcliffe tonight. Your men are discomfited by my presence." She glanced over his shoulder at the men who refused to look at her. They searched the ground, stared into the distance, and turned away.

"Doctor Radcliffe," he amended and offered a supportive arm. "There are hollows in the ground covered by dead grass and it's easy to stumble, let me escort you across the field."

She waved away his offer and began to walk toward the group of officers. He didn't express his opposition to her attendance at this scene but there was no doubt he believed her presence wasn't natural. Instead he accepted her graciously and led her silently to the victim.

The woman lay cold upon the hard frozen ground, her clothes ripped open to expose her savaged body. Rowena clenched her teeth, and held back molten bile as it rose into her throat. As a doctor, she had seen death before. Nevertheless, it was a struggle not to cry out or release the flood that stung her eyes.

She gathered her skirts close, and carefully lowered herself to examine the wounds. She took shallow breathes until she was prepared for the mental challenge of the task she'd come to do. Record the evidence that lay before her. The killer's abandoned prey highlighted his excessive hatred and rage. The woman's chest was crusted with blood, entrails were carelessly discarded, organs sliced away.

Finally, having completed as much of the examination as she could, she rose. "Have you found a weapon?"

"No. Nothing. I've had the men search the grounds. They've done as well as we can expect tonight. We'll do continue to look when it's light."

Rowena glanced back down at the young woman. "Have you been able to discover who she is? What may have brought her here?"

"No, but in a small area like this, it won't take long to learn who her people are."

Rowena nodded in acknowledgement of his words, surprised at the sadness in Layne's voice.

"I can't imagine what kind of monster we'll discover when he's found." He turned away from the scene. "We have a lunatic. No sane man could do this thing."

"Unfortunately, I cannot agree this is the work of a lunatic. My studies have revealed some of those who commit the vilest murders fully understand what they do is wrong, but believe it is their right to do as they please."

"Surely you don't think this killer is such a man."

"I am afraid to say I believe just that. You are aware there have been several similar killings over the past few months, the last in Newcastle."

"Are you implying you think more women have been killed by the same hand?" Layne shook his head, his face pinched in disbelief.

"I am."

His words rushed out in objection. "No killer could do this and escape from justice."

"I won't be sure until I have examined her in better light, but I believe there is one killer. He travels across the country, selecting and butchering women and she crossed his path."

Layne stared at her, eyes wide, shaking his head in denial. "You must be wrong. You must."

Rowena didn't answer. Though she prayed she was wrong, she believed she followed the trail of a single killer.

———

CHAPTER ONE
March 1888

Rowena shivered. The nights were still cool and the dense fog only added to the chill. The mist had a way of insinuating itself into her heavy cape and clothing, leaching all the heat from her body. She prayed the journey would end soon. Not just the trip, for they were already pulling into the courtyard of the inn. No, her prayer was that this voyage into the darkness of men's minds would end quickly.

The coach slowed, and then stopped. Her driver opened the door.

"Fagan, I hope you find comfortable quarters here, I know you long to reach home as much as I." It felt good to stand after the crushing ride.

The man shrugged as he assisted her from the coach. "Thank you for your concern, my lady. I'm honored to be at your side."

She smiled weakly as she walked to

the door, wishing the steps she climbed were to her house in London. One more day and she'd be home, but the journey was too long to complete tonight and she'd agreed to the meeting. Lord Bradley Sheffield had sent her a message and was waiting for her arrival.

"My lady," the innkeeper bowed, "I was told to expect you. Your rooms are almost ready."

He led her toward a table beside a cozy fire burning brightly in the dim room. Candles created small pools of light on the tables. Though electric light lit the entry hall, the innkeeper had clearly decided the tavern would profit from the old style ambience.

"Perhaps you'd have some refreshment while my wife completes the arrangements?"

"Thank you, a bowl of hot soup would be appreciated, along with a glass of red wine," Rowena said as she glanced at the people seated about the room.

"Right away my lady. I'll tell Lord Sheffield you've arrived. He's been asking after you."

She sank into the chair, gathering her cloak closer when the heat from the fire failed to reach her. Wearily she took in her surroundings. A sprinkling of locals sat about the room. Two old men smoked pipes and nodded their heads in agreement at the bar. A young couple smiled, chatted, and held hands a few tables away. In the corner, directly across from her a man read a newspaper and sipped from a tankard.

The scents of the day's meals lingered enticingly in the air making her realize how hungry she was. She smiled when a young woman brought her soup, wine and a generous portion of fresh bread and placed it on the table. Feeling better as she ate, she smiled again when a burst of hardy laughter filled a corner of the room where several men sat. Looking at them her smile faded when she recognized the man who appeared to be looking in her direction sitting at the head of the table.

Damn, what's he doing here?

She averted her gazed from the group, praying the man hadn't recognized her. She realized her wish was unanswered as he rose and walked toward her.

Rowena wasn't prepared for the encounter and could feel her heart pounding so hard she was sure he would hear it. She struggled to maintain a calm facade as he stood towering over her.

16

"I hear you're still playing the part of the dedicated woman of medicine," he drawled as he looked down. "I don't understand the fascination you have with death and those who kill."

He slipped uninvited into the seat beside her.

"De Grey. I hoped it was a doppelganger sitting across the room. What cause do you have to accompany such rowdies?" She could feel her irritation rising as a lazy smile spread across his handsome face.

"I find you a challenge, my lady," he said. "I'll enjoy watching when you fail this task Albany has set. I can't imagine why a man such as he would believe you could do anything to stop this villain *if* there is one. Albany has many loyal servants willing to take up the chase."

Rowena clenched her teeth, but found it impossible to hold back the retort, "de Grey, you're a fool. You'll crumble to dust before I fail. I'll be there to laugh at your demise." A flash of memory flared recalling a name of affection she'd call him in the past.

His eyes gleamed as he called the proprietor to the table.

She studied him as he took his time

placing his order and talking to the man he apparently was familiar with. She couldn't stop herself from comparing her memories to the man he had become. His hair, thick and black, fell across his high forehead and over his collar, longer than most men wore it. His cheekbones were more pronounced than she remembered, and his square jaw had a more determined set. As her eyes took in his broad shoulders she began to imagine how he would look without the suit coat and shirt hiding his muscled chest. She had to force herself to remember she no longer cared for him as he turned back to her.

"Bradley Sheffield will be along shortly. Do you really wish to join us?" she asked, forcing herself to look into his eyes.

"It might be interesting," he said calmly, though his tone belied the tension between the two men.

Rowena glanced across at him, uneasy. Garret de Grey and Bradley Sheffield didn't attempt to disguise their hatred for one another. Their bitter disagreements had spanned years.

What am I doing here? Rowena wished she would awake to find this was only a dream.

"I see you have no desire to talk,

but let me say I think you're beyond your capability," de Grey taunted. "If there *is* a man killing women as he travels across the continent."

Despite being furious he could still make her react. She leaned forward and hissed, "You're no more than an irritating fool and would do better to rejoin your friends. You won't win at this game you seem set on playing, whatever it is."

The landlord's daughter delivered de Grey's ale. The girl didn't linger as she set the drink on the table quickly, then slipped silently away.

Rowena sat back, glancing toward the doorway, hoping Sheffield would finally appear. Surely, he would force de Grey to walk away. Since the day Albany granted her wish, de Grey had been somewhere in the background. She had been able to avoid a direct confrontation before tonight.

"Go away, Garret. I have no wish to trade insults," she said, unable to keep the weariness from her voice.

De Grey studied Rowena, "I understand you are returning from Oxford. It must have been difficult see the man hanged. And more difficult to have the the men in the village shun you since they find your involvement unfitting."

"It is *most* difficult because the one they accused and hanged is the wrong man. He was a weak-minded fool who confessed to something he didn't do."

"Can you be so sure?"

"Yes, I am *sure*. He didn't have the anger to have done such a thing. He was a simpleton who allowed those stronger than he make him confess."

The door opened and Lord Bradley Sheffield stepped into the room.

"Sheffield's arrived and I have business with him," she said, relaxing a bit as she dismissed de Grey with a wave of her hand.

Taking his time he drained the tankard and set it on the table before standing. "I'll leave you to your meeting, but I'll remain close, Rowena. I'll be near until the end of this foolishness."

She felt empty as he left, and she watched him stride toward Bradley Sheffield. *I won't care. I can't care.* She closed her eyes hoping the action would make his face fade from the place it held in her mind.

———

He could feel Rowena's eyes on him as he crossed to the center of the room where Sheffield stood smirking.

"Garret de Grey, I see you've come to toy with our lovely doctor. You should grow up. Stop taunting her and trying to make Albany think she's incapable," Sheffield laughed darkly, causing several people in the room to turn, shifting uneasily in their seats.

"I don't know what your game is, Sheffield," de Grey said through clenched teeth, keeping his voice low. "I know you're not here to help Rowena."

Sheffield's eyes seemed to glow as he looked over at the woman sitting by the fire. "Our lady doctor doesn't seem to have the same opinion. She sent me a message asking that I allow her to join me here for a little chat. I couldn't refuse."

Garret studied the man standing before him, wondering why he was lying about something so meaningless. He knew Sheffield had asked for the meeting. One of his men had been the one to deliver the message.

It unsettled him that he felt jealous as he realized he was comparing himself to Bradley's handsome looks. He had to admit the man's dark hair and broad shoulders would make a woman lean on him, but such things had never impressed Rowena in the past. Perhaps it was the aristocratic, outrageous sense of humor that drew her to him, though Sheffield's outlook on life wasn't so uncommon among the privileged. Personally, he found the man disturbing and hated knowing he had such easy access to Rowena.

"What pleasure do you get from this? You don't go out and look at the horrors created by this madman. Nor do you seem to offer her support when she believes there has been an injustice. What game are you playing?"

"Actually, I find it all highly entertaining." Bradley smirked and glanced over at the men sitting at the table beside the bar who were watching the exchange closely. "I believe you're doing the same," he sneered then stepped around de Grey to join Rowena.

Garret returned to his table but didn't join in the conversation. Instead, he watched the man and woman beside the fire. Night and day. Rowena's golden, flame-kissed hair glowed in the dark room. Sheffield was a dark shadow against the gloomy walls.

He called for another drink and turned away, hoping no one would notice how much he still cared for the woman across the room. Once he'd believed she was the one person who would come to love and understand him. He had been wrong.

"She's a beautiful woman," the man sitting next to him said. "I bet when you look in her eyes you see fire there."

De Grey shook his head. "No, you see ice, and it will turn your heart cold."

———

"Sheffield, good to see you even though it is a sad occasion," Rowena said as he sat across from her. "I've just come from seeing a man hanged for a crime he didn't commit, and I was powerless to stop it."

"Why should *you* be sad? He was just a lunatic." Abruptly he changed the subject, "I've checked your accommodations and find them passable. Tonight you should rest, perhaps stay an extra day, we can find *something* to distract us in this godforsaken place."

"No, I'm anxious to get to my house in the city. At least there I can relax." Glancing across the room she said, "I didn't know de Grey would be about. I suppose he's on some mission to escape his responsibilities again."

23

Ignoring the comment, he said, "It was cruel of Albany to allow you to take on this quest. I don't understand what he thinks you can accomplish."

"It was a favor I asked of him. I'm hoping to gain insight into the heart of this killer. You're aware I studied prisoners in New York during my medical training and have since worked in France and Germany. I learned so much about how they think, of what they are capable. I want to put that knowledge to use."

"Yes. I'm aware of your penchant for doing what would cause other women to faint," his word spilled out touched by sarcasm. "I admit I *was* surprised when you decided to become a *doctor* of all things. You really had no need to do that. You've lands, a title; you should be planning balls and teas."

"I do what's right for me, what I'm compelled to do by my heart."

She studied the way his eyebrow raised in disbelief, and the smirk that touched the corner of his lip, wondering why he only made her want to laugh when he patronized her, while de Gray made her want to claw and bite.

"I admired Elizabeth Blackwell's ambition, her drive to become a doctor, so I took the time to do the same. I was honored to attend her medical school. She's changed the world for many women and provided me the ability to play my role here in England."

"Ah, perhaps it makes a kind of sense, but it's too much like work. Then I've never really understood you have I, Rowena?"

"Nor have I ever been able to comprehend the workings of your mind. Yet we appear to be friends."

"So tell me, what makes you believe the death of these men isn't justified. I find it rather fascinating. Being hanged for something you didn't do."

Rowena took a sip of wine to hide the disgust his words evoked. "You're too interested in the dark side of people's lives. I don't know why I tolerate you."

Sheffield waved at the waitress, appearing to only half listen.

"In all the years, I've known of your fascination with things others find horrifying, tonight you've finally surprised me," she said. "How can you laugh or see any humor in these matters?"

"Life is quite boring if you follow all the rules, my dear. I'm interested in those who can't or don't follow in the footsteps of the masses. Most people are like sheep, no will of their own, afraid someone will think badly if they sneeze at the wrong moment."

Bradley stopped talking as the young waitress delivered the requested drink.

When she left he continued. "Don't you find these men you question more alive? More assured what they do is the only way it should be? How can you not admire them, want to know all you can? Is my interest less acceptable than yours?"

Rowena sat back, her disgust deepening with what she'd just heard. She'd known Sheffield since they'd been children and though he always had a more unkind view of those he considered menial, she'd never found him so callous and cruel.

"The look on your face is *priceless.* I actually made you speechless." He cackled as he applauded her reaction. "I've tried for *years* to create that concerned expression on your face."

Rowena wondered if she really knew the man sitting across from her.

"You've always had such a gentle and generous heart," Sheffield drawled. "I feel it's my duty to make you better understand this cold world we live in. I'd begun to believe you were beyond being shocked by anything I might say or do."

Unsure how to respond, she shook her head. "Sheffield, I admit I never quite know what to expect from you."

"The worst, darling. Always expect the worst and you'll rarely be disappointed.

—

CHAPTER TWO
April 1888

Rowena looked up as the door opened, grateful to have an excuse to stop studying the reports that lay on the desk in front of her.

The drawing room was large but comfortable with its warm wood paneling, Regency Mahogany Pembroke table, Hepplewhite Carver chairs, and gilded chaise lounge. The floor was covered with a fine Persian rug that had been part of her home since before she was born. She rose from her desk and walked to stand in front of the settee as His Grace the Duke of Albany entered the room followed by members of the Metropolitan Police. Rowena excused Margaret after she brought the tea and set it down on the sideboard. Albany introduced her to Dr. Robert Anderson, the Assistant Commission of Scotland Yard. Anderson had the military bearing you'd expect of a man who had spent many years in command at various stations throughout the kingdom. One could easily imagine him holding a pith helmet, a monocle to his eye, and dramatically clicking his heels.

Chief Inspector Donald Swanson, Anderson's assistant, was younger and less stiff in his bearing. He had a pleasant face sprinkled with freckles, and green eyes that held a sparkle of humor. She noticed how careful he was to assure Anderson took the lead before accepting a seat at Albany's request.

"My lady, I've directed these men they will willingly assist you in your hunt for the one you believe is murdering women in our countryside," the Duke said as he settled into his seat. "However, I must warn you, neither of them shares your opinion that the men punished for these crimes were wrongly accused. It's their feeling the men hanged for these horrors have served the cause of justice."

Rowena smiled. "I know my idea is not a popular one, but if you'd seen the victims and the men who were condemned for these deeds...they couldn't have committed those abominations. I've spent time studying criminals in prisons here, in America and France. The men accused of these murders may have been violent, but they didn't have what I'd term the fervor for such fury."

Albany extended his hand to accept the tea she offered. "I believe you are convinced of what you say and I am willing to help you either confirm the truth of your words or discover you are incorrect. To help you in your quest I brought these men to meet you in the hope they will understand who you are and why you feel so strongly in this matter. Regardless, they will support your investigation.

He turned to address the men.

"Lady Radcliffe has worked for many years to understand the damaged mind of men who kill. Her work is renown among those who conduct similar studies and she has convinced me she should be permitted to delve into matters similar to those that have already occurred in other areas of the realm."

"I can't think of a reason in the world to believe this theory," Dr. Anderson criticized, "and even if it's true, the Yard and City Police will make short work of him."

"Perhaps," Rowena said, "However, I still wish to be involved if something should occur. You may think me alarmist, but I hope you'll be open to let me assist. We can learn so much about how a killer thinks, how his mind works and put that knowledge to use."

Dr. Anderson pursed his lips, glanced at the Duke gauging his demeanor. "Go on."

"I believe it's possible to determine what type of person is capable of taking human life in the most horrid manner, and then use this information to weed through the suspects. In America there is a study of what the scene of the killing tells about how the murder occurred, as well. I want to learn what I can and it is my wish to be called should anything occur."

"All the information we need from the scene is the name of witnesses. Then it takes a great deal of talking and observing to determine who the villain is," Anderson blustered.

"Yes, that seems to be the consensus among many of the police, though a few are beginning to incorporate some of the findings of my colleagues into their work," she said.   "However, I'm not asking you to accept these theories, just allow me to study the people and places of the killing."

"I hope you're wrong, and no such killer is here in London," Swanson stated. "But surely, you are not asking to be present at the crime scenes and don't wish to actually see the victims immediately after discovery?"

"That is precisely what I want," Rowena assured him, glancing at Albany who gave a slight nod. "I believe that's the reason you were brought to meet me."

Dr. Anderson sputtered, apparently horrified at the idea of a woman at a crime scene. Glancing at Albany he ground his teeth before commenting. "You'll be called should any such horror occur but we must agree on the specific circumstances. We cannot invite you to every incident. You must also understand you will *not* be listed as an official part of the investigation. The world would be horrified to learn we even talked to you of such matters. No, your name will not appear on our records."

Swanson gave a small smile, and she could see the light of mischief in his eyes, but he didn't speak.

"Thank you Doctor, I'm grateful for

any privilege you can accord me, and you must know, I do hope I'm wrong."

Lord Albany satisfied that Anderson would do as charged, changed the subject. "So, my Lady, how does your women's society go?" I understand you have opened a surgery for the care of the impoverished men and women of this city, though I believe they're not worthy of your generosity."

"It goes well, Your Grace," she said, careful to hold in the retort that readily rose to her lips. Albany and so many of the peerage held themselves above the people who worked to eke out a living of any kind, failing to understand their privileged circumstances were just an accident of birth.

"There are many who are generously willing to help every day. Last year I sent two young women to America to train under my mentor, Dr. Blackwell. They are due to return soon," she said.

"It's an admirable ambition, but you can't treat all who may need your services," Albany said.

"True, but we're beginning to gain the trust of the men and women forced to live on the streets. I've even had some success in convincing a few of the

33

workhouse bosses to call me when someone is injured rather than just tossing the injured person out on the street. I've assured them the other workers will see them as benevolent and work harder. It's difficult but rewarding."

"Well, I wish you the best in your enterprise even if I don't understand why you're so concerned," Albany said. "However, I am concerned about the reports I've received recently. I'm told you roam the streets at night searching for those who hawk their bodies to others. You put yourself in danger's way."

"I appreciate the concern, Your Grace, but I must do what is best for these people. They're more afraid of me than I of them, and they need care, just as others do."

"You *are* a caring woman, Rowena. I hope that driver of yours stays close as you make your rounds. He's a fearsome looking fellow and will discourage the rabble."

He stood abruptly, indicating the meeting was over.

"Well, we must go."

The other men stood as well.

"Come round to the Yard later and I'll introduce you to the Detectives,"

Swanson offered. "It will make it easier for them to know who they're dealing with should there be a need to call you in."

"Dr. Anderson, Chief Inspector Swanson, thank you for coming." Rowena walked around the desk and offered her hand as they said their goodbyes.

It was hard not to react to the disapproving look the doctor gave her as he tepidly took her hand and bowed unenthusiastically. She didn't want to offend him as he could make it very difficult to learn what she must, if her fears proved to be true.

———

The small waiting room held the women needing her attention. Several of them looked at her with suspicion as she walked through to the examination room, but were willing to allow her to do what she could based only on what their friends had told them.

"Good morning, Ellie, I see you're back to have the dressing changed on your leg. Have you been keeping it clean?"

"I, 'ave been, lady. Washed it up good jus' two nights ago." Ellie sat on the edge of the examination table and lifted the edge of her dirt-streaked dress to allow Rowena to see the wound.

Rowena studied the young woman. She had been surprised when Ellie told her she was only fifteen. Rowena would have estimated her age closer to thirty. She was frail and bent with the weight of poverty. Thin dirty blonde hair fell in clumps about her sun-darkened face which bore scars from the battering she had taken during her short life.

"Fine," Rowena smiled and gently removed the wrapping. "It's healing well and the infection's gone. I don't think I need to see it again if you continue to follow my instructions."

Ellie nodded, watching carefully as Rowena worked. She washed the area and put salve on it then measured out a small portion for Ellie to take with her.

"You tell your Jacob he's to be more careful where he leaves his tools. Now, is there anything else I can do for you?"

Ellie shook her head, and gave Rowena a gap-toothed smile. "Nah, I be good and I thank 'ee for 'elping me. Em were right about ya'."

"I'm glad you think so. Tell your friends, if they need medicine I'm here to help." Rowena handed the small jar of ointment and a few coins over to the woman who nodded and rushed to open the door.

"Use this cream two more nights. If the cut begins to redden again, come back and see me," Rowena called after her.

"Aye, lady," she said, stepping quickly out the door.

The rest of the afternoon was more of the same, cuts, bruises, and a catalog of problems that, for the most part, were easily attended. Rowena closed the office early, intent on attempting to find several of the women who had not come in as requested. Some worked in the mills and factories. Others lived on the street or in the hovels called common houses. These were the poorest women and men, those who couldn't afford to miss time from the horrible places in which they slaved. The factory bosses and owners made it clear the workers were dispensable. Thousands of people searched daily for work, even if it was for only a few hours, to help feed themselves and their families.

Once these unfortunate souls began to understand she truly wanted to help, it had been easier for them to accept her care, but she had to constantly seek them out to follow up and assure they were doing as she urged.

Then there were the women who

traded their bodies on the streets at night. They frequented the worst pubs and taverns hoping some drunken sailor or laborer would pay for a few moments of *service*. It always amazed her how these women could justify their livelihood. They were much harder to convince she meant no harm, yet with time even they had been convinced she wished to help.

———

Rowena exited the last workhouse on her list, and decided she should take the time to see if any of the others she sought were working the taverns tonight. Fagan followed at a distance as she started up the dark street. She didn't want to give up the hope of locating a particular young girl who'd come to her several days ago, though she suspected the search would prove futile.

Rowena walked down the narrow lane holding her head high. It was dangerous to look insecure on these streets. Though many of these people knew her, it did not guarantee her safety. She wanted them to believe she wasn't afraid, but even with Fagan following her, a trickle of fear always grew as she searched the dark alleys and streets.

A soft groan drew Rowena's attention. A woman, who at first glance appeared to be no more than a bundle of rags, was slumped in the doorway. Kneeling close to examine her, she was greeted with the powerful stench of rotted teeth and cheap ale. A quick look assured her the woman was only drunk and had no obvious injuries. Rising she continued her tour.

"'ey lady," a lad of no more than sixteen years called out as he walked toward her, stroking the crotch of his filth-covered pants. "Got wa ya need rite 'ere."

A second boy stepped out of the shadows, whispering something to the first. The lad stopped then abruptly tuned and ran the other way followed by his friend.

"'e wone bother ye," an emaciated old man called out from the alleyway. "O'are would skin 'im if he touched ya." His crackling laughter turned into a hacking cough. "Leave me be," he gasped as she moved toward him. "Doan want yer tendin'."

"Even if I can help?

"Why? Make me live longer on these gold-covered streets." He laughed until he choked.

No. From the sound of your cough I

39

don't imagine I can keep you alive much longer. She gave him a few coins, and moved along. She continued toward the faint light leaching through the grime-covered windows of a pub.

The door opened and the shadows eased a bit on the street as a sailor and one of the prostitutes stepped out, blocking Rowena's way. He stood staring at her with bleary, suspicious eyes until the woman pulled him away from her and together they swayed down the street holding each other up.

She walked past the door, up the dark stretch of street. Several times she stopped to speak to someone standing in a doorway, or crouched in an alley, offering medical assistance only to be turned down every time. Finally, crossing the foul-smelling ditch to the other side of the street, she made her way back to where she'd started.

"You're more fool than I gave you credit for," a deep voice said from the shadows.

She searched the darkness. "De Grey, what are you doing here at this time of night?"

Rowena slowed as she approached the man who leaned against a wall until she could make out his features.   He scowled at her, his eyes unreadable in the dark.

"Are you searching out favors from these poor women?" She knew he wasn't but couldn't keep from being snide. Whenever he appeared, which had been too often since their meeting at the inn, she was sure to say something outrageous.

His lips twisted into a chilling smile.

"I could ask a similar question of you. Why would a lady of your stature be out walking these dark streets at night? But then I know your answer," he said, standing straighter and looking down at her.   "Your quest to make life better for these pathetic creatures is an obsession. I'd heard you had a penchant for these unseemly promenades. I thought I'd come confirm for myself how foolish you are."

A door opened, pale light spilled out on the street as another pair of drunks stumbled into the misty night. When they noticed Rowena and de Grey, they stood swaying, uncertainty showed on their faces.

"Wa' ya doin' 'ere?"   The man bellowed as the woman tried to hush him. Turning to his companion he shoved her hard against the bricks of the tavern wall.

"Woman, leave me be."

De Grey stepped forward, towering over the man.

"You've no need to treat her so. Get out of here before I show you how such treatment feels."

De Grey's voice was soft, but held the promise of his words. The man didn't question as he half ran, half stumbled out into the dark night.

"Wa' ya do tha fer?" the woman whined as she launched herself away from the wall. "He'd a paid me, now wha 'm I ta do?"

Rowena stepped closer. "I'll see you get money if you let me treat you. The cut on your face where you hit the wall could become infected."

The woman looked her over carefully, assessing her clothes and the way she talked.

"I 'eared 'bout you. The lady doctor, been goody, goody helping us girls here on the street."

"Yes. Do you have a friend who's been to see me?" Rowena smiled as she set her bag down and collected the materials she needed to clean the cut.

"Aye, Annie says ya be alright." Looking over at de Grey, "Maybe yer man wants a little sample wha' I got? I'll only charge 'im double," she cackled.

Rowena shook her head, smiling at the crude joke. "You might spoil him for others," she chided dabbing cream on the wound.

Taking the woman's hand she placed a small jar of the salve and several coins in her palm. "Now this money is not for drink," she warned. "You make sure you wash this cut and keep it clean and put this cream on it daily. Use a bit of the coin for food and hide the rest for harder times."

The woman's eyes were round in awe at the amount of money she held. She nodded silently.

"I'm Doctor Radcliffe, Come to my surgery if you need help or if the cut gets swollen or red. Do you know where it is?"

"Yeah, Annie showed me one day. It's over by the George Yard buildins."

"Right, now...what's your name?"

"Mary, me lady."

"Well Mary, go home, spend a safe night in your rooms. No need to find a friend for tonight. Your work is dangerous, but now you have the money to see you through for a few days."

Mary made a poor attempt at a curtsey as she agreed, then turned and ran toward the street where her companion had disappeared earlier. Rowena hoped she'd get off the street for the night but wouldn't wager on it.

"You did that well, she'll trust you again if she has need," de Grey said stepping out of the shadows wall where he'd stood silent, watching the exchange. Reaching out he offered to carry Rowena's bag as she lifted in from the ground.

"Perhaps." She shifted the black doctor's case to her other hand away from de Grey's reach. "I find it difficult to believe you're interested in the services I provide these women. If I hadn't seen it with my own eyes, I would never have believed you would go to the rescue of that poor woman."

He shrugged. "I admit I'm more interested in the woman providing the service than her patient. However, I saw no reason to let the lout beat the woman up in front of you. You've always been a fool for the less fortunate and I believe you would have tried to stop him if I had not."

"Those are almost kind words, de Grey. Are you feeling unusually sentimental tonight?"

Ignoring her sarcastic words, he glanced past her, his lips curved into a wry smile. "I see your watchdog is anxious for you. You should keep him at your side. After all, you don't know who may be about and intent on harm."

Not waiting for a reply, he turned around and walked swiftly to the end of the street, disappearing into the thick fog.

Rowena watched the spot where he had vanished for a moment. Was de Grey warning her or threatening her? She rubbed her arms as a chill ran up her spine. Having done all she could for one night, she returned to her carriage and instructed Fagan to drive her home.

Her carriage moved out of the dark streets. She had to admit de Grey's sudden appearance had shaken her. Though he said he didn't believe her theories, he had taken the time to remind her that a vicious killer might be out there, somewhere in the dark. As the wheels thumped along the street her mind reeled with questions. *Was she right? Was there a single killer striking down woman in England? Was he in London? Would he strike soon?*

―――

CHAPTER THREE

"Bradley, what brings you here?" Rowena, surprised at his sudden appearance at the surgery she tried to gauge the reaction of her patients gathered in the waiting room.

"I was hoping I might find an elegant lady to have tea with me this afternoon." He glanced around the room at the women who stood staring at him. "You've told me so much about the work you do, I thought I'd come see for myself."

She glanced down at the timepiece pinned to her blouse. "I have a few more patients to see before I'm free. Perhaps I can join you somewhere when I'm done," she suggested, hoping he'd agree to leave.

She really didn't appreciate his sudden appearance and worried the women would be intimidated by his presence. "You should have let me know of your interest and we could have arranged for you to come by at a...time I'm not so busy.

"I'll wait," he smiled and tipped his hat at the group huddled together in one corner of the room. "I'm sure your ladies won't mind."

The women glanced at each other then burst into robust laughter. "May 'ap ye take us all ta' tea, me lord," the boldest suggested, standing and raising her skirts so he could view her naked, grimy ankle. Swinging her hips, she strutted forward.

"I fear our good lady doctor would be most unhappy if I chose your company over hers today, but perhaps I can sample your charms at another time," he said as he lowered himself into a chair, settling his hat on his lap.

Rowena, surprised at his words, stared at him for a moment, wondering if he'd really meant it as a joke.

Ridiculous. First I think de Grey is threatening me, now I'm wondering if Sheffield means to connect with one of these poor women for carnal pleasure.

Dismissing the idea, but still suspicious of Sheffield's sudden appearance, she invited all the women into the examination room.

Bessie, the quietest of the group, was battered and bruised, her face having connected with the fist of one of her customers.

Rowena gently cleansed the open wounds on her cheek and forehead then picked up the pot of her special salve. "I hope this isn't the same fellow who abused you so before," she said as she applied the ointment to the area around Bessie's eye.

"Aye 'twas, my lady. 'e pay good money fer the service I give and 'tis nothin' to worry you so."

"Men shouldn't use their fist on you Bessie. I thought we talked about this before."

"Yeah, but me da' always took 'is fist ta me when I be bad, same as 'e did me mum. It's a man's right."

Rowena was sure Bessie and the others believed what was being said. She could heal their wounds but no amount of talk had been able to change the women's minds about what a man had a right to do to them, especially in exchange for money.

She turned her attention to Lizbeth to treat the wound that had resulted when she was stabbed in a fight with another woman. They had been at a tavern in search of customers, each claiming the attention of the same sailor. "You need to make sure you keep this clean, Lizbeth.

Are you using the soap and salve I gave you?'

"Was doin' but I was tossed out of me room for lack of rental. Gov would na take the rent in trade neither. Sad day for 'im."

"Well, I'll give you a new supply, but you best carry it with you. I'm sure you have some place to store these small packages on your person."

Lizbeth grinned showing the gaping holes where her teeth should have been, "I do mum."

"Then be sure to carry this with you and treat your wounds as I've shown you." Glancing at the last name on her list she asked, "Now Rose, what is it you need to see me about?" This one was much younger than the other two and still had a look of youth about her. Although somewhat yellowed, she had all her teeth as far as Rowena could determine, and was cleaner than most of the women she tended.

"Tom, over to the mill said I should see ya when I wernt posed to be workin. I...," she lifted her skirt to reveal a burn mark approximately two centimeters long. The skin looked charred.

"What happened? Did this occur at

you work?" Rowena had the woman sit down and placed her leg in her lap, for a closer inspection.

"Nah, did this last night at the 'earth, got to close and mostly got me dress on fire. Lucky Mandy 'ad one to lend me so I could go to work this mornin', but I put in me twelve 'ours and Tom Said you be good enough to take a look."

"I'm afraid this is going to hurt when I clean it. If you need to scream or cry you go ahead. I'll be as gentle and quick as I can." With that Rowena scrubbed off the top layer to find healthy red flesh below.

She admired the young woman's stamina as the work progressed. Though tears rolled down Rose's cheeks not even a moan escaped her lips. "There now. You keep this covering clean for two days before you remove and change the dressing. Run clean, and I mean very clean water over it, before putting on the ointment, don't scrub at it again until I've seen you."

Finishing as quickly as she could, she escorted her patients to the door and offered them her standard gift for permitting her to treat them. If money was all they understood, Rowena was determined to use hers to assure as many of these women stayed as healthy as possible in these harsh conditions. Her friends had been concern that she would be at risk of inviting one of the less honorable men or women in the area to try to take her coins. She had almost rejected the thought without due consideration, after all it was just a few pennies a day for each of the sick and injured but then she realized those pennies looked like a fortune to people who had nothing.

Fagan was on guard outside the office, but that wouldn't protect her if one of the patients was determine to take more than their share. Again it was O'Hara who spread the word that he would not tolerate theft or injury of his Lady Doctor. Even so she only kept enough to pay two or three patients at a time on hand when she was working. The rest was securely locked in the safe where she could easily access it between visitors.

No matter, even if she was forced to give away all the sums she possessed, it would be of little consequence if she could help these people and give them a better life.

———

"I'm sorry I kept you waiting, but I

have to ask, what are you doing showing up here like this, Bradley?"

"I was bored. I decided to surprise you at your home, but was told you were working. I just had to see it for myself."

"You are growing too bold," Rowena snapped. "It's inappropriate for you to be here. I've worked hard to gain the trust of these people and your appearance could-"Why are you so upset, they're just riff-raff, I'm not likely to scare them away. Do you have a favorite place for tea, or shall I choose?"

Rowena bit back the anger she felt knowing anything she said would be a waste of time and energy. "Your choice."

"Then it'll be Grosvenor's. I enjoy their tea cakes more than most."

Collecting her things, Rowena locked the door to the small office and instructed Fagan to return home before silently joining Sheffield in his carriage. Sheffield didn't seem to notice her irritation as he chatted on and on about the latest gossip.

Arriving at the tearoom, they were seated and Rowena spoke for the first time since leaving the surgery. "What are you doing here in London? I thought you'd have taken off on more travels. I know how you detest being bored."

"I decided to stay here when I learned you'd be in town. I thought we would join forces and cause an uproar among our friends. It has been a long time since we were both in town at the same time."

"What would I have to do with your decision? I'm tired of traveling and want to build my charities. I thought your new game was to drag your cousins about and show them the wonders of the world as you did last year?"

"Yes, I did, it was a bit of a lark," he chuckled. "However I found them boring as well," he said.

Rowena smiled at her wayward friend. "I did have a difficult time picturing you running around the continents as part of some aristocratic pack."

"It does create a sort of challenging pictorial don't you think. They're so callous and self-absorbed, that's what I found so enticing when we began the travels. Anyway, for a while they entertained me."

Rowena relaxed and smiled at the thought he found others callous and self-absorbed when he was both.

"We're both considered a bit unusual to our peers, Rowena. However, you may note our friends adore that which they don't understand. They think I'm particularly useful to lift the drudgery of the day and require my presence at all the best parties," he said.

"I'd never have believed you'd come to this. I'd never expect you to be interested in carting young lords and ladies on your travels then entertaining those who wish to put you on display at their soirées."

"How often do we find the time to just dally and enjoy what's around us? The youth of the cousins re-opened my eyes to the wonders that abound. Besides, I had Morgana Ridley with me to nurse them and remove them from my sight when they annoyed me," he said removing his gloves and setting them in his lap.

They were silent as the waiter delivered tea, placing cakes, scones, clotted cream and jam on a table between them before he filled their cups and quietly walked away.

"You introduced Morgana to me in Oxford," Rowena said as the waiter walked away. "I hear she's still with you, which surprises me. You don't need her to help you escort children about the world if you're staying in town."

"Morgana's a novelty, so until I grow

tired of her company, I'll find something for her to do. What about you? When will you take time to relax and enjoy doing what you wish?"

"I've seen more of the world than one would wish," she said thinking of the horrors she had seen on four continents. "I've found something here I care about, the help I can offer the poor. I like the way I feel about myself, and enjoy what I can do to ease the suffering of others. It's a good life."

"It's an odd life. You should find a husband to settle you." Ha! Sheffield dismissed the seriousness of her words with the wave of his hand, turning serious attention to the tower of sandwiches and sweets before he made his selection.

"Well, enough of this talk of dark and ominous matters. Are you planning to go to Lady Ormondes' ball next month?" Sheffield sipped at the tea, watching Rowena over the cup's rim.

"I've an invitation, but I'm not sure I want to go. These gatherings begin to blend and become tedious after a while."

"How right you are, but you really *must* put in an appearance. I'm sure you could use the time to draw some wealthy individuals into your charitable little web," he teased.

She laughed. "I'm not a spider. I really haven't given it much thought."

"Then you should have a proper escort and at least make an appearance, my lady. You will cause quite a stir."

"Are you asking me to go with you?"

"Splendid idea," he said, his face brightening in feigned surprise. "You must go or you'll dash my dreams into the ground. We're the two most outrageous and gossiped about people in London, and we'll arrive as a couple. I can't wait to tell them how fine you look in your little office giving care to those horrible, foul women. We'll have such an entertaining evening."

———

CHAPTER FOUR

A fine mist fell outside the windows and fog rolled along the streets discouraging trade on the night streets. Many of the *Ringers* patrons had been there for some time. The women huddled in a corner of the room, watching the activities taking place in the pub.

JohnT threw darts and almost hit one of the men sitting beside the board, his aim getting worse the more he drank. He'd already lifted more than a few pints. Billy Rocket yelled at a mate across the room, making a wager on who'd get a job the next day. Pearly'd come in and left with a sailor.

Weak candle flames flickered, fighting for oxygen as the room filled with customers smoking pipes or cigars. An outsider might have turned away when he opened the pub's door to step in. They'd be met with an assault on the senses. The smell of unwashed bodies, stale beer, and things best left unnoticed, filled the small, low-ceiling room along with the peat smoke from the poor fire in the hearth. The pub owner's wife was boiling potatoes and what smelled like old shoes to serve to those daring enough to eat.

"Did ya deliver the note? I can't believe she's gone all uppity in the world. She's gonna pay." Mary Jane asked Kate, cackling with excitement as she sat with her friends having a pint.

"I give it to the butler. 'e looked at me like I was some kind of vermin, but 'e took it on that platter 'e was holdin'." Kate snickered, sipping a bit of rum. "Where be Mary Ann tanight? I swear there be too many of you Marys"

The women all laughed and nodded their agreement as they raised their tankards to their missing friend.

"She 'ad to go off, but'll return later."

"Bet she wonders 'ow I found 'er. There she be jus' strollin' down the street bold as ye please," Mary Jane lowered her voice so her words were covered by the noise of the others gathered in the room. "Followed 'er to that fancy house she's livin' in. Would a thought she owned it, way she went right in the front door."

The women nodded, understanding exactly what she meant.

"Ladies, I promise I'll share when I gets what's due. She's gonna pay fer the things she done ta me. She's gonna pay and pay well so I'll 'ave enough to find us all nice lodgins. "

"Mary Jane, you take care," Annie cautioned. "I wouldna' be happy to find my long lost and have 'em makin' demands. She don't know where ye' are, but you'll 'ave to meet when ya' collect, so be careful."

"It's not the lodgins I'm wantin'. I seen a dress 'd look lovely with me eyes," Mary T joked. "I'd love ta have a new fancy dress jus' once in me life."

"And so ya kin have. You ladies gave me the idea, and it's a good un, so we'll share in the profits. She can afford to help us do better and she will," Mary Jane assured her friends.

"What you want most, Annie? Ya been quiet tonight," Kate asked the small woman with the blue eyes that crinkled at the edges.

"I be wantin' ta get meself out of 'ere, and find a little place where me children will want to come see their mum. I do miss 'em."

"Least ya know they're out there, not like me children who drowned on the *Princess Alice*," Liz said sadly.

"Which children they be, Liz? The nine ya never 'ad?" Mary T asked with a roar of laughter.

Liz grinned. "It be a good story for some. People take pity on a poor widow what lost all 'er children and a 'usband to boot. Problem is I ferget who I tole what and ya 'ave ta be careful when dealin' with the charity. They got long memories."

The women nodded agreement and broke into giggles.

"So Mary Jane, what we gonna do now?" Kate asked the woman sitting next to her.

"We're gonna let her stew a bit, best to let the pot simmer, then we'll be tellin' 'er where to come to make the first...donation."

The five women raised their glasses in silent agreement.

———

Rowena stripped off her gloves then removed her hat as she stepped into the main building at Scotland Yard where she'd agreed to meet Chief Inspector Swanson. A Patrol Constable stood ready to direct her to the correct office, but asked her to wait until a second guest joined them.

A door in the hallway opened, de Grey stepped out.

"What are you doing here? I thought I was meeting Swanson," she said, biting back the annoyance she felt at his sudden appearance.

"You are." de Grey smirked. "And I've been asked to join you."

"Why? What do you have to do*" Rowena stopped, questions would get her nowhere and she didn't want to fight in the middle of a police station.

His smile widened.

"Fine. I can't imagine what your interest is in this, but now isn't the time for such a discussion. I don't want to keep Donald waiting," Rowena whispered through her teeth.

"This theory of yours is so fascinating. I admit I am anxious to see the reaction of the detectives when you are introduced."

"I can't understand how my ideas are interesting enough to take you away from your *friends*. You've never been concerned with police activities before, unless it was avoiding their grasp."

De Grey's eyebrow rose as he looked at her. "Haven't I? Well, these are unusual times. I told you I'd be close, and though you may not admit it, you may need my help."

Turning toward their guide Rowena offered a smile. "I believe we're ready, is there a special place we're to meet?"

"I was told to direct you to the CID building in the center yard. If you'll allow me, I'll walk you over."

They followed closely as he led them out of the main office. Three buildings formed a "U" and the criminal investigation department sat in its own building at the center of the other structures.

Chief Inspector Donald Swanson was waiting for them, seated at a large, well- worn desk when they entered.

"I'm happy you decided to join us, my lady. I'm sure you don't mind me including Lord de Grey in today's tour."

"Of course, as our gracious host you may invite whomever you wish. I appreciate you've given me this opportunity."

"Wonderful. I have a couple of Detective Inspectors I want to introduce to you. Around here we call them DI's. They're fascinating fellows. You'll find their methods of investigation most modern I'm sure." He led the way to a small room where several men sat in deep discussion.

"They are dedicated to finding criminals. If you have the unfortunate occasion to meet with one, they will follow the trail, no matter how slight, until they locate the offender."

"I've heard good things of the men who work for the Metropolitan, though I understand it is now called Scotland Yard," Rowena said as she looked around the room.

Surprise had her call out to one of the men. "Inspector Layne, you're a long way from Oxford." She smiled as he came over and she introduced him to the two men.

"Doctor Radcliffe, I didn't think I'd see you again. I hope you aren't investigating another death," he said, looking over at one of the men he'd been talking to. "Abberline, this is Doctor Radcliffe, I told you about her. She thinks we hanged the wrong man back home after that horrible murder."

Abberline was a tall, reedy man with a high forehead and receding hairline. His thick mustache swept across his face into his mutton chop sideboards. As he walked over to join them he eyed her intensely, making her just a bit uneasy.

Rowena offered her hand.

Abberline smiled. "Layne told me a lot about you. I believe you have some interesting theories on crime."

Swanson stepped forward as another man walked across the room. "Ah, Lady Radcliffe, Lord de Grey, this is DI Andrews. Lady Radcliffe and Lord de Grey are interested in the study of the criminal mind."

The group chatted for a few minutes about current investigations and the use of photographers in police work. Layne excused himself as he was due to leave and return home.

When he was gone, Swanson turned back toward his detectives. "I want to make it clear, if we've any assaults, murders that appear to be in *any* way similar to what Layne had in his backyard, *Doctor* Radcliffe is to be notified immediately. She has the authority to attend the scene of crime and view the bodies in their *unmoved* state."

"Possible we may be seeing each other again, though I truly hope you're wrong," Abberline spoke in a serious tone. "I have to admit I'm skeptical there is one killer and he's coming to London, but I'm open to seeing what happens."

"I pray I'm wrong," Rowena admitted.

The detectives escorted Rowena and de Grey around the grounds, talking about the different functions of each of the areas that housed the police force. They stopped at the evidence room, where materials from crime scenes were housed, and looked over some of the more unusual items being held, then made a quick pass through the jail.

"It's more complex than one would think," Rowena said as they returned to the CID building. "So many people are involved in these investigations at so many different levels."

"Yes, and we're lucky here," Andrews assured their guest,"smaller towns and villages don't have the history or the equipment we have to help us in our work. We even have phone stations about town so the PC's, that's Patrol Constables, can call in from their area when something happens that requires our attention."

"Lord de Grey," Abberline stopped and turned toward the man he addressed, "you have been quiet today. Do you have any questions about what you have seen?"

"The tour has been quite

informative, but the test will be watching you in action should the occasion to do so arise."

Rowena watched the men, as they seemed to size each other up. It wasn't like Storm... *Where did that come from?* ...it wasn't like *de Grey* to challenge an officer of the law, but his tone...

"Yes, well we'll see what happens," Abberline said. "It has been an honor to have you both here. I'll call the desk and have someone meet you at the door to the main office," he offered to Rowena.

A PC ran in with a message for the detectives from the front desk.

Andrews took the note and scanned it quickly. "Is this all there is, PC Pender?"

The young constable shrugged. "All the information we've been told."

"Seems there's been an assault down near Whitechapel Road," Andrews advised them as he put the note in his pocket.

"When is there not?" Abberline asked as he took his coat from the back of a chair. "Is she dead?"

"Don't know, but since it doesn't say, I assume she's breathing," Andrews answered.

"Perhaps I can assist," Rowena

said. "I *am* a doctor and if the unfortunate woman needs help, I'm may be able to give a hand."

"Come ahead, then." Abberline shrugged. "Can't do any harm."

"We'll go in my carriage," de Grey said, inviting himself along.

"If you must." Rowena followed the detectives from the room. As they were about to step into Garrett's Brougham she stopped. "Just stay out of my way, Garrett. I want no part of your games."

———

CHAPTER FIVE

It took longer than she would have expected to reach the site of the assault. They had to go down Commercial Street near Dorset and the carters lined the street with their barreled goods, flowers, fruits, and vegetables from the farms. The center of the street held carriages waiting for the merchants to make their selections, forcing the traffic to a standstill.

They worked their way slowly off to the side street, where de Grey ordered his driver to go around the cloth market, which was filled with sample materials and clothing made in the sweatshops. For such a poor part of town, there was an overwhelming display of activity during the day, yet at night these were the most dangerous streets in London, abandoned by all but those forced to live here.

They found a small group of men and women huddled together speculating about what had happened, when they arrived. Inspector Andrews called out to one of the PCs as Rowena and de Grey approached, "Pitman, move these people back."

"My lady," he said leading her to where a woman was propped against the wall of the mud-stained building. "I don't think your services will be much needed. Though she shows some damage I believe it is minor."

Rowena took her time examining the woman. Her limp brown hair was matted with blood where she'd hit her head against the uneven brick wall before sliding into the position she now sat. Her clothes were torn and cut in several places. Although a bit bloody, there was no indication there were any life-threatening wounds, though you couldn't always tell.

"Do you know your name?" Rowena bent over the woman, relieved to find her somewhat coherent. It was obvious she'd been drinking and was still inebriated.

"Pearly Poll they calls me. Wha ya doin? Leave me lone." The woman tried to stand but fell back.

"I need to look at you, see what injury has been done." Rowena looked over her shoulder at the men huddled around them. "Gentlemen, can you arrange for some privacy, please?"

Pearly's laugh echoed through the alleyway. "Gentmen? 'Rivacy? Yahr daft."

Rowena waited until the men turned away, and then gently lifted the soiled skirts. The wounds appeared superficial.

"These need to be cleaned and treated, but I don't believe you're in danger from them if they don't get infected. You should go to the hospital though and have the wound on your head stitched up," she said, promising herself she would carry her bag with her at all times in the future. She could have taken care of these cuts had she had it with her.

"'ospital, naw." Pearly slapped Rowena's hands away and struggled to stand. "I doan go to naw 'ospital." Her struggle became weak as she drifted into a faint at Rowena's feet.

Stepping over to Inspector

Andrews, Rowena requested the woman be sent for treatment and gave him a brief description of the minor injuries she'd observed.

"Do you want to go to the hospital and treat her?" de Grey asked as she stepped out of the inspector's way while he gave instructions to call for the ambulance as Rowena asked.

"No, the hospital will give her adequate treatment. There are several wounds, however they don't appear to be severe."

"Well, then tell me what benefit there is to have you here. You are at a crime scene, your medical skills aren't needed..."

"Perhaps not, but I have learned quite a lot since we left Scotland Yard."

"Such as?" de Grey quirked an eyebrow at her.

"To begin with, this is not where she was attacked. It may be difficult to find the site of the original attack as the onlookers have walked over any evidence that may have been available before we arrived."

"Why do you believe she wasn't attacked here?" Abberline, who had overheard her, asked.

"There isn't enough blood.

Although she had minor wounds there would be traces around her if she was stabbed here in the doorway."

"That could be significant I suppose," de Grey agreed," but what difference will that make in the investigation?"

"It will be difficult for the police to find witnesses if she walked here and doesn't give them the information they will need to find where she was actually attacked."

"Yes, you are correct, My Lady," Abberline said as he joined them. "You are as observant as Inspector Layne led us to believe, so perhaps your presence won't be a total waste of resources as some in the department believe."

———

It had been an eventful day, but not in the way he'd expected. He'd only accepted the invitation from Swanson to irritate Rowena and show her he could be anywhere she was at any time he chose. He enjoyed the flash of anger in her eyes when he appeared unexpectedly. Yet his heart had beaten heavily in his chest when the detectives had agreed to let her go to where the prostitute lay injured. He hated she would want to see such a sight, and more that she could be invited to do so.

He lifted the tankard and allowed the ale to slide down his throat, praying it would quench the thirst that possessed him.

"You look angry" His companion motioned the young serving girl to bring another round of drinks. "Is there something special of note I have missed?"

De Grey looked at Finnegan, then at the other men sitting around the table. "I'm just tired of waiting to see what she'll do next. The *lady* doctor is irritating."

The men had accompanied him on several excursions into the dark of night as he had tracked her wanderings through the streets at night. None of them really knew why he seemed so intent on keeping an eye on the woman, other than she was beautiful, but society had many beautiful women, all beyond their grasp.

"Lord, you seem in an ill humor. Perhaps tonight we should find some other method of entertainment."

Slamming the tankard down on the table, he rose. "No. I find I have tired of your company and whining. I'll take time for myself tonight. You can stay here and get drunk should you wish." He words may have sounded harsh, but the men were unaffected. They'd soldiered at his side, were loyal and true friends who understood his moods. The three, Finnegan, Stovall and Skinner would be available should he need their assistance later.

He had his driver take him past her house, but all was dark as it should be at this hour of the night. He kept telling himself it didn't matter what she did, what she would do, but he knew it was a lie. He ached to reach out, hold her, protect her, but that would have been the very thing to make her turn away. At least for the moment she was tolerating his presence, though she was not as graceful about it as she might have been.

Arriving home, he went directly to the library, intent on reviewing the finances of his properties, a tedious job that would require concentration. Such a job should distract him and keep his mind off her. Yet he found it almost impossible to make sense of the numbers on the pages before him. As he looked all he could see were her eyes, her lips.

Determined to cast her out of his mind, he pulled more papers from the drawer and stared down at them for several minutes before pushing away from the desk and walking to the sideboard to pour himself a drink. The too-large house was quiet, the servants all tucked into their beds. He looked up to see his grandfather staring back from the frame above the fireplace, a knowing smile on his face.

You certainly put me in a bind, you old rascal. I'd never have gotten in the Queen's sites if it hadn't been for you.

His father and grandfather had spent their lives in special service to the royals, and as he had come of age, the expectation had been he would follow. For a short time he had balked at the idea, ignoring the summons whenever he dared, then Albany had appeared.

Glancing at the clock, he realized it was almost dawn. Setting the drink aside, he walked to the window, searching the dark sky. Was she right? Was there one man killing the women they had found mutilated across the country? Was he here in London or on his way? It made a horrible kind of sense, knowing what he did about the death of the three women. All of them slashed, tortured, mutilated in various manners. Would three separate killers be possessed to create something so similar?

Rowena had always had an uncanny sense when it came to the

darkness of a man's soul. When they'd been younger, he'd often been amazed at how accurate she'd been; recognizing those of their own set who had a black heart.

I thought she was addled when she told me she could feel the evil in Martin Dunning.

Yet only a few days later he'd been discovered drowning his sister's kitten. Lord Dunning had laughed, called it a childish prank, but others had been horrified and the family was stricken from the invitation lists that season. A year later Martin was found standing over a young servant girl he'd strangled and raped. He'd been spirited away in the night, and no one but his family knew where he'd been sent, but the fact remained, Rowena had been correct.

Pushing the thoughts away, he went to his rooms to prepare for his meeting with Albany. He shouldn't care about the vile women who had been murdered. What difference did they make in the world? Yet something stirred in him. He'd seen the horrors that had been done. He'd talked to the doctors and police in the cities where the tragedies had occurred. He knew the killer was a monster beyond anything the world had seen before.

If, he's here in London if, he's begun a hunt for his prey, the city will feel the effects for years to come.

—

CHAPTER SIX

My lady, you've a package in your study," Margret said as she placed a tray on the table in Rowena's dressing room.

"Thank you Margaret," Rowena said as her housekeeper gathered the tray from the evening before. "Was there a return label?"

"Yes, your friend, Doctor Blackwell in America."

"Wonderful." Rowena dressed quickly, anxious to see what treasures she would find from her friend.

In her study she gathered the package and went directly to her desk and carefully cut the strings binding the package. Inside she found reports from jailers, police investigators, and several men doing research on the behavior of killers they had observed.

Doctor Blackwell had penned only a short note, identifying some of the sources of the materials and wishing Rowena luck in her studies.

It had been a surprise, when she had first become interested in the minds of predators, that scientist and doctors believed information could be gathered from individuals or the scene where assaults and murders occurred. More surprising was how many of the police, so closely involved in those investigations, were uninterested in the ideas being offered.

Doctor Bradley Faulds in Tokyo had written an outstanding journal item detailing the use of fingerprints as a method of identification. Faulds even proposed a method to classify the prints so they could be compared to others at a later date. Many other scientists had written of their personal collections and theories of their use in searching for murderers. But the only identification of a murder suspect using this tool to date, had been in a *Life on the Mississippi,* written by the American author Mark Twain,

Knowing speculation about the methods of identifying people would get her nowhere, she returned to reading the report details.

There appeared to be a number of things many of the killers had in common, once you found them and were able to ask questions. They believe killing is normal and others in their situation would do the same. These killers appeared to try to bully and intimidate anyone having authority over them. More unsettling was their sense of superiority, often leading them to taunt the police as they committed murder, before their capture.

The reports the package held were interviews with the men who had committed a series of murders before they were caught. Some of the reports included a word-for- word detailing of the answers the murderers had made to the questions they had been asked. The apparent casualness of the replies was chilling although she was aware of the lack of conscience these people possessed.

Rowena studied every page, comparing several of those that had the most detail, before compiling her report to the society for crime she had joined when she was doing her studies. As she worked she lost track of time and was surprised when Margaret knocked on the door to announce the arrival of the new doctors from America.

Portia and Lucinda had not grown up with the privileges Rowena had, but had learned to read and write as members of the households where their parents had worked. They had been destined to continue service for the aristocracy, as tutors and nannies before Rowena had been introduced to them by one of the women who took an interest in her Medical Society for the Poor. Both women were eager to learn and be of service to others. After a series of interviews, Rowena had sponsored them, sending them to Dr. Blackwell in America as candidates for medical training.

"Lady Rowena," the women said in unison as they curtsied after being shown into the office.

Rowena laughed. "Why are you being so formal?" She walked around her desk taking each lady in her arms and giving her a hug before stepping back to look them over. "It is hard not to see how your confidence has grown," she said.

"Look at the way you hold your heads up and the smiles on your faces. I had a letter from Dr. Blackwell and she insists you did outstanding work during your studies."

"Oh, but it is so good to be home, Portia said.

Rowena indicated they should be seated before she again took her chair at the desk. "I'm sure your families are glad to have you back as well."

"Everyone is fine and they gave us such a welcome home. Lucinda's mother broke out in tears when she came to my parent's cottage."

Lucinda laughed. "She did, then wanted to know why we hadn't met some nice young men and married, But she was just trying to hide the fact she is worried about our commitment to you. We want to go to work just as soon as possible but the families think we will be in danger."

"I will do all I can to assure you are not placed in the way of harm. You will both work with me at my surgery while we are preparing yours. When you go out on your own, you will have someone like my Fagan to watch over you and make sure you are always safe," Rowena said.

The young woman began to talk excitedly about the plans for the surgeries and the experiences Rowena had already had in working with the poor. By the time tea was served, Rowena was just as excited as they were.

———

The surgery Rowena had furnished for Portia and Lucinda was only a few short blocks from her office in the George Yard Building. The space sat at the corner of Brick Lane and Fashion Street at the edge of the most violent district of Whitechapel. As close as the two offices were, in this poorest section of London, they could have been miles apart to the people they were there to serve.

On the first day the new office opened, Rowena was there to help as a trickle of patients arrived. The word had spread as they worked at the original office, but many people were reluctant to have her protégés assist them if they could get to her facility. Her presence made it easier for the people living in the area to accept the services at the additional location, and she already knew several of the patients.

"Jackaman, I'll see you first," she called as she opened the examination room door. "How's your foot?"

"Better every day, mum. I see ya

83

has respect for a man, takin 'im in before the 'arlots."

"I've always had great respect for you. You served in the war, did you not, and kept our home safe?"

The old man grinned. "Many a war mum, I fought in them all ya know."

Rowena smiled, although he may have done some service at one time, he had certainly never been to war, but it was a tale he liked to tell. It was more likely he'd been one of the dock workers most of his life, but she would never voice her doubts.

"O'ara sends you word, you're young ladies er safe. 'e 'eard you was there this mornin' and wanted ya to know fer sure.

She changed the dressing on the old man's foot. "Thank you Jackaman, you can take a message to O'Hara as well. I thank him for his care of my new facility and the women who work here."

"Ye earned 'is respect when 'e got cut. Yer didn't scream fer the billy clubbers to come to yer side."

She laughed. "I doubt it would have done any good, surrounded as I was by his rowdies."

O'Hara.   No   one   had   trusted

84

Rowena when she had arrived in these dark streets and said she was there to help. Initially, if it hadn't been for Fagan, she would no doubt have been assaulted or killed. All that changed when a ruffian, Kelsey O'Hara, had been stabbed during a brawl. One of his henchmen rushed to her office, almost dragging her to the injured man. O'Hara recovered, and from that day he'd given her protection. He was extremely influential among the gangs and bullies who roamed the streets day and night.

She finished wrapping the clean bandage over the cut. "There you go. That should keep you for a few days. Come back when the bandages need changing again and try to use the crutch we gave you to keep the pressure off your foot."

Aye lady," he called, ignoring her instructions, as he scurried through the door. It amazed her how agile the old man was, even with the cut on the bottom of his foot.

Calling in the next patient, a young woman who had just recently arrived in London, she gathered the bandages and materials that would be needed and prepared to serve as an assistant to Portia. Though this was only the girl's second visit,

Rowena knew her all-too-familiar story. She'd been forced into the hardship of life on the street when her family could no longer afford to keep her and their other children under one roof.

Trina, barely fourteen, was petite with thick, clean black hair that hung down her back. Freckles covered her nose and big violet eyes still filled with innocence watched as Portia began to work. The sunny disposition she'd had when Rowena had met her just two weeks ago was already taking on a sharper edge, but she could see the hope for better things still glowing in the girl's face.

"You've done a fine job of keeping the burn on your hand clean. I don't see any signs of infection, and it appears to be healing well," Portia said.

"Did everything you tole me, lady doctor. I made sure I changed the bandage like you said and put on that cream you give me."

Rowena asked, "Have you had any luck finding a job in the factory, or the warehouse I told you about?"

Trina looked down at the floor, and shook her head. "But I met a gentman who told me 'bout work in France. Said it was a fine place."

"What kind of work, Trina?"

The girl answered quietly, "Not nothin' you' be wantin to hear about, but it sounds so fine and over there it be legal to...work."

"You're not talking about a brothel? I've heard there are men about who recruit for them."

"Doan know you call it, but he tole me about all the money ta be made, fine clothes, fancy house ta live in. Not like 'ere where you sleep in the street or share a room wi' a drunk."

"He's lying to you, child. There are no such wonderful places for the kind of work he offers."

"But he be a proper lookin' gentman. Didn't do or say nuthin' bad ta' me. Dint even ask me fer a kiss." She wiggled as she smiled.

"Perhaps, but I've been to France. I know the kind of places they house young girls to do this work. People like him make fancy promises then sell you to do service."

Nah, can't be. He offered ta' buy me clothes and a ticket fer the trip. Said I could go back wi' 'im next week."

Rowena watched as a clean bandage was wrapped over what was left of the burn, wondering if there was anything she could say to make the girl understand the offer was a fantasy. Looking up she could see sadness reflected in Portia's eyes as she worked.

Deciding to change the subject, she smiled. "Did you mother come into town? I know you were hoping to see her."

"If she did, I don't know. She'd tole me she would come but even if she could I doan no 'ow she'd find me. The grocer 'ad no note fer me, an she said she'd send one for she came."

"Well I'm sure if you have patience she'll come when she can."

"I might be gone."

"So you're considering going with this man?" It saddened Rowena to think the child would follow this procurer, but she knew Trina had little desire to do more with her life. She'd offered to place her in a school to learn to work as a domestic, but Trina had only smiled sadly and refused. Perhaps she didn't have the confidence, but Rowena suspected the life of a servant was no improvement to the child over the life she was already leading.

"I'll surely think on it, 'bout wha' ya tole me, lady. I'll think real 'ard. Kin I go now? I'm ta meet a frin."

"Yes, we're done. Take care Trina,"

Rowena called as the girl ran out the door, not even waiting for the coins she should have received for returning to have her hand looked at.

"She's going to go, isn't she?" Portia asked. "I can't imagine why. It will be horrid in a foreign land, no friends."

"Yes, I think she'll go."

"Is there something we can do, go to the police perhaps?

"I'm afraid it would do little good. It's my understanding, from someone who understands these things the police see it as a way to rid London of unwanted people. There is no crime committed as these girls go voluntarily, and the men can't be arrested for lies."

"I hadn't realized how heartbreaking this job would be. So many of the people who come are young and inexperienced in life, yet they find themselves living in the harshest conditions."

"You're a wonderful woman, Portia. You have such a kind heart. I wish there was more we could do, but... I don't see anyone else waiting, why don't you go ahead and go home? I'll take care of the office and close up."

"You don't want me to dwell on the girl." Portia forced a smile. "You are the one with the heart. I'm just grateful I have you to lead me and help me learn."

"Well, go on. Perhaps you have time to do a little shopping for that new dress you've been talking about. If I remember correctly your young man will be home in a week or so."

Portia blushed. "Yes, the naval office confirmed Josh would be here soon. We have permission to be married upon his return. The letter came yesterday."

"Wonderful." The door to the street opened and another patient stood in the waiting area. "Go on, I'll take care of this." Rowena smiled as she watched the young woman collect her things and walk out the door.

Rowena called out to the woman who had just entered, and went back to work. She tried to set aside the sorrow she felt for Trina, and prayed she would come to her senses.

Slowly more patients arrived and left the new facility. She worked past teatime before closing the doors. Now that the people knew the surgery was open, and had met the doctors who would regularly populate it, she was satisfied she could leave it to them.

Portia and Lucinda would staff this

office tomorrow. Lucinda would open the doors to her facility in a few weeks after the word had spread about the care she and Portia were providing.

Night was swiftly approaching when she finally closed down. Fagan waited in the outer room, faithful in his duty to shield her, as she locked away all the supplies in a heavy vault she'd purchased just for that purpose. She may have personal safety guarantees, but the closed office was an open invitation to anyone who wished to invade and remove the tools or medications left out unprotected.

—

CHAPTER SEVEN

"It's good of you to have us back so soon. I had hoped we'd be able to talk for a bit during our last visit." Rowena took the chair Abberline indicated, while de Grey sat in the one beside her.

"I wanted to discuss your theories as well," Abberline admitted. "I am interested in the things Layne told me while he was here."

"Well I'm most interested in how you do your job. How do you go about deducing whom is the person you need to arrest?" Garret asked as he shifted his chair. "I've read some of the chapter stories in the paper, but the processes used in some of them are rather outlandish."

"I guess you've read that book of Doyle's with his drugged-up detective Mr. Holmes. I personally have never had an appetite for cocaine nor found it particularly useful in my work. Nor have I a magnifying glass that I carry with me to the scene of the crime." Abberline gave a wry smile as he turned back toward Rowena

"So, what questions do you have, my lady? I'm sure there are many."

"There are and I suppose the first is most basic. How do you investigate? It seems to me there are so many people involved in the hunt. I'm not sure where you'd start."

De Grey raised his eyebrow and she wondered why. Was he also interested in the question or did it mean something else?

"It's not an easy thing to do, but with the phones we've located about the city it's easier to get earlier notification. In the past, the officers had to run and find a second constable who then ran to the nearest station to alert the detectives when they were needed." Abberline glanced at a report as a constable handed it to him, then continued. "Often the scene of crime was cruelly destroyed by the time I or one of the other DI's would arrive. Even now, it may happen this way in some areas of town."

"Wouldn't it be more efficient to have two men patrol together?" de Grey asked.

"It would, however, it would cost twice as much to patrol and the citizens would not be happy to have to pay for such extravagant service."

"So your victim is found, you have been notified, what then?"

"I hope the PC has detained a few of the witnesses for me to talk to. They are the most important part of our investigation, to a point."

DI Andrews appeared at the door. "Found the note asking me to join you. Good day my lady, my lord."

"Come in, we were talking about investigating a scene of crime."

"That can be quite a chore." Andrews smiled and took a seat on the opposite side of the table. "Or it can be so easy you can't believe your luck. You'd be surprised how often the felon is caught with his hand in the till or leaves so much information about himself you feel sorry for the poor old chap."

"So now I have two questions based on what you've just said." Rowena looked at Abberline. "What do you mean witnesses are good to a point? And DI Andrews, explain your last statement as well."

"Go ahead, Andrews," Abberline insisted.

"You would be surprised how many of the criminals are so pathetic they leave their papers lying about or tell the witnesses their names or even walk up and offer to be witness to the crime.

Had one walk right up to me after he stabbed a poor chap and took his shoes. Fortunately the shoes' owner didn't die, but the man who stole them offered to witness. He had wet blood on his pants and was wearing a very distinctive pair of custom shoes on his feet." Andrews roared with laughter at his own story.

"In answer to your question about my saying witnesses are good to a point," Abberline said to Rowena, "I admit I don't often find one as helpful as the chap Andrews was talking about. I find witnesses are very unreliable the longer it takes before you have a chance to talk to them. With a significant delay they'll make errors in their statements or forget details of the event."

"I heard the same from police in New York when I was there. They rarely trusted what they were told."

"I'd suspect the anxiety of discovering a crime might be a reason for such poor ability to recall the events correctly," de Grey mused.

"Perhaps. I think it's more that people don't really pay attention to what is happening around them, then try to fill in the faces or events, to make us happy with the tale they tell," Abberline stated. "So tell us about your knowledge of killers, gained from your investigations into the minds of men in prison."

"You say that as though you think I'd be uncomfortable expressing my beliefs," Rowena challenged. "I do believe the men who I met in the prisons have a lot to tell you about others who kill."

"You're not going to go off into some story about how they have been abused by life? I've heard that tale more than once and find it difficult to accept," Andrews stated. "There are many people who live a hard life and don't take the lives of others."

"No, Detective Andrews, I had no intention of going down that path, as I too have heard almost every man I met in prison claim they're there only because of the circumstances of their birth or some grave mistake. The things that interest me are more subtle. The way certain of these men seem to have no honest feelings. They may act as though they feel, but usually they are only imitating others around them."

"How could you determine that, Dr. Radcliffe?" Abberline sat forward in his chair, interested at last in what she was saying.

"I'd interview them in groups of offenders. Some were obviously echoing the reactions of the others in the group, when a reaction would be appropriate. It was not always so obvious but you find a few. When I wanted to be certain, I'd remove them from the group and interview them over similar but varied subjects."

"You weren't alone with these men," de Grey growled. "The Warden of the prison wouldn't allow such an outrageous experience."

"No, I never visited these men without the presence of a guard or two. However, I always coached the guards on the questions I'd ask and how I wished them to react. It was interesting for me to observe who imitated the guards in this setting or who responded as though the stories I told, of harm to others, were just a form of fanciful entertainment."

"I still believe the warden who allowed you such access should be drawn and quartered," de Grey huffed. "You had no business being so close to those men."

"I find your information fascinating, but is it really of any use?" Abberline asked turning toward Andrews. "Can you think of a way we can use such information?"

"It makes little sense to me," Andrews replied. "My lady, I really can't imagine why you'd even want to study such things."

"To discover more about the nature of humans, humans who are capable of killing and have no remorse for having done so. Do you think they're just average men who have crossed a line? I don't, nor do others who study them. We believe there's something lacking in their basic nature. If you know what to search for when you meet them, you'll be able to identify them for what they really are. Monsters among men."

———

Rowena watched silently as Garret stepped into the carriage and sat across from her. The conveyance pulled away from the curb with a familiar jerky start as they sat in silence, the only sound the clip-clop of the horse's hooves and rumble of the carriage wheels on the stone.

Garret gave her a wry smile before he spoke. "You have interesting ideas, but I don't think you should be involved if the killer begins to make his mark. I admit I have serious doubts we'll see his handiwork," de Grey said.

"I don't understand why you think you have any right to voice an opinion, Storm." Rowena stared across the aisle of the carriage. "You suddenly appear in Germany six months ago, and act as though you know what I'm involved in. You follow me, or appear to, through Newcastle outside Oxford and turn up here participating in meetings I've set up with the Commissioner of Scotland Yard."

"I care about what happens to you," Garret sat forward reaching toward her as if to take her hand, wondering if she realized what she had called him.

Placing her hands on her lap, she glared at him, daring him to touch her. "Why should you care? I haven't seen you in three years. The whole time I was in America you never wrote, or . . . you have no right."

"Row, I-"

"Do *not* call me that," she said through her teeth. "You lost the right to call me by that name years ago when you worked so hard to waste your life." She fought the tears threatening to form as she remembered what they'd had. Turning to look out the window, she bit her lip.

"As you can see, I haven't wasted my life. I am still quite the man I always was." He leaned back in the seat. "You didn't understand what you were seeing back then and you took off without a word."

"I took off? You're the one who disappeared. I waited for six weeks without a word from you. Aunt Carla asked me to join her on her trip to visit her daughter, Dora. I accepted."

"Then stayed to attend that school and look at you today, Doctor Radcliffe, Countess of the street urchins."

Rowena pounded on the ceiling of the carriage. "Get out. I don't know what possessed me to allow you to travel to this meeting with me. Get out and stay away from me."

"I'm sorry."

"Sorry doesn't even begin to describe the man you've become. I don't know what your game is, de Grey, but I refuse to play it."

They stopped. Rowena could hear the driver of the cart behind them, screaming obscenities at Fagan.

"The road is a busy one, de Grey. Get out and let me be on my way."

His face was stone as he opened the door and dropped to the ground. "My lady, we'll be meeting again, and soon. You best find a way to deal with it, Albany has asked my help and I intend to honor that request. You won't get rid of me so easily on future occasions."

She wanted to scream, but wouldn't give him the satisfaction of knowing how angry she was. Angry she hadn't remained cool and calm. Angry she hadn't brought him to his knees, begging forgiveness for his rude demeanor and past hurts. Angry she was lying when she tried to tell herself she didn't care.

She watched him walk to the curb, before she signaled Fagan to proceed. Albany was the cause of this, though she couldn't imagine why he'd want them to have to work together. It really didn't matter. Nothing mattered more than finding a killer who was invisible and silent. A killer no one else believed would appear.

———

CHAPTER EIGHT

The day had been much too long, and after the scene with Garret, she was in no mood to have to attend some fancy ball. Yet she'd accepted and it wasn't worth a fight with Sheffield. She'd no doubt he'd pout and drive her to distraction if she decided at the last minute to back out.

Margaret announced Bradley was waiting in the parlor. Knowing she had delayed as long as was reasonable, Rowena checked herself in the mirror. The woman looking back at her showed no signs of the exhaustion and disenchantment she felt. Her hair was pulled straight back with a simple braided bun atop her head accented only with a small jewel embellished comb. She hated the feathers and hats of the period, electing to ignore the custom of wearing them. She buttoned her gloves before picking up her fan and evening bag.

The dress she'd chosen was of the finest verdigris colored silk and changed her eyes from icy to a softer, more marine blue. The cut enhanced the regal stance she'd been trained to adopt by nannies and governesses through the years of her childhood. She motioned Margaret to gather her cloak and took a deep breath before facing the first challenge of the night. She plastered a smile on her lips and glanced a final time at the mirror. Satisfied she descended the stairs.

"You look lovely tonight." Sheffield took her cape from the maid and set it around her shoulders. "You're capable of dressing in style, I see. You'll be my most beautiful trinket this evening."

Rowena laughed lightly. "I told you I'd do my best not to embarrass you. I hope you're not planning to make this a long, tedious night. I'll put in an appearance, a bit of dancing will be fun, but I'd like to return home early."

"We'll see what the night brings." He held her hand as she stepped up and took a seat, then followed her in and sat across from her.

The ride to the Ormondes was brief but they had to wait as the carriages in front of them dropped off their passengers. Rowena breathed a sigh of relief as they finally arrived and entered the brightly lit house.

"I see you're fashionably late," Lady Ormondes teased Bradley as she turned to his escort. She puffed up like a frightened cat when she realized his companion was Rowena. "Lady Radcliffe," she managed to keep her voice carefully cordial, "I admit surprise you accepted my invitation. I wasn't aware Lord Sheffield would be your escort."

Rowena ignored the implication as she looked around. The Ormondes' house was aglitter with lights and candles. Hundreds of flowers were set on tables in the hallways and in each of the rooms she passed on the way to the mirror-lined ballroom. The women were dressed in their finest gowns and jewels, and a current of excitement ran through the room. Many of the young women were making their first appearance in society. By the end of the season, they'd wonder why they'd been so excited, though some would be planning their weddings.

Walking into the ballroom Sheffield leaned in close to whisper, "I knew you'd be the talk of the ball. I was certain we'd cause quite a stir, and *you* already have."

"Behave. The Ormondes have no reason to snub me, as you well know, at least not as long as Albany acts as my mentor. She's just upset she has to have someone in her home who attends those who have *lost their way*. Perhaps she believes I will adopt the behaviors of those I care for."

"I've attended some of her card parties. She does think you a wicked and evil woman for giving those people care. Of course she never actually mentions your name, but it is obvious she means you and the women you've had educated."

Looking over the crowed room, Sheffield smirked. "I see de Grey is among the guests. Ah and there are my young traveling companions, Percy, Bradford, Grace, and Fiona. Excuse me a moment, I'll have a word with them."

Rowena didn't need to answer as he was already on his way to the far corner of the room, where two young women stood making it obvious they were trying to ignore each other. Apparently, after having traveled together, they hadn't remained close friends, but it was no concern of hers. The young men rushed to Sheffield's side as she moved slowly about the room, stopping occasionally to speak to those who had her acquaintance.

She hadn't attended many of these gatherings in the past few years, though she actually enjoyed dancing and quickly accepted the offer to do so. Lord Smelton was entertaining, babbling on and on about his excursions into the world of shipping.

Lord Albany honored her with a sweep about the floor before handing her off to Sheffield, who gossiped about the young men and women he'd sought out when they'd arrived. "The girls seem to be quite jealous of each other. Apparently the Marquis's oldest son danced with both of them and well...they appear to be set on assuring only one of them wins his further attentions," Bradley said.

"Sheffield, you delight in the most uncomely situations. You shouldn't encourage them to behave so badly."

"Rowena, it's their parents and nannies who should correct their abominable behavior. I'm just an outside observer."

"And have no influence over them, though they traveled at your side for more than a year. Never mind. I think I'll step outside for some air. Go torture some other damsel with your gossip."

Sheffield laughed and promptly disappeared in search of another dancing partner. She made her way slowly to the French doors where she could step outside and enjoy the moonlit gardens. As she passed a group of women one of them called out to her and she stopped once again.

"Oh, I'm surprised you're here," Baroness Botlesford piped as she squinted and assessed Rowena's gown, frowning. "Lady Radcliffe, we were just talking about your charitable efforts. I just can't imagine how you can stand to touch those people," she said in a voice that sounded like a mouse squeaking.

"Baroness." Rowena gave her a forced smile. "You should attend my surgery some time. You could then carry tales of your good deeds to your friends."

Lady Botlesford's eyes bulged at the suggestion. "Yes, well, I am sure you do good works, but..."

One of the women Botlesford had

been talking to distracted the woman with a question which allowed Rowena to escape.

Just as she thought she would reach her goal, a gloved hand caught at her arm. "Lady Radcliffe." Marchioness Ulster smiled warmly as Rowena turned toward her. "I see that harridan Botlesford was giving you a hard time. I hear good things of your venture to help the poor. I've wished to call upon you, but I only returned last month from our house in the county. I'd love to learn more about your work and see how I can help."

"I admit it's nice to hear such kind and encouraging words. I'm not well received by many of the ladies here tonight."

"Most of them are brainless fools." The Marchioness laughed. "I'll have you to tea next week and we can talk of your work, compare opinions of those who bait you."

The Marchioness' words buoyed Rowena's mood. "I'll look forward to your invitation."

"Here, come and join me for a small bite of Lady Ormondes' buffet. I admit I failed to dine as well as I should before we arrived, worried my gown would be too snug. I do love these delicacies and tend to often over fill my plate. Oh, well, what else is there in life that brings so much pleasure?"

Rowena laughingly agreed and followed the plump, energetic woman into the room where a buffet of every imaginable confection was laid out for the guests.

Picking a few of the canapés from the overloaded platters and placing them on her plate, she and the Marchioness talked until the Marquis came in search of his lady.

"Cecil, you know of Lady Radcliffe, do you not?"

The Marquis took her offered hand. "You're the one Albany talks of so highly. I understand you're actually a doctor, is this true? Quite amazing for one so beautiful."

Surprised, Rowena laughed. "I am sir, though-"

The sound of voices raised in anger interrupted the conversation. Stepping to the ballroom door, Rowena saw the two young women Sheffield had pointed out earlier in the most distasteful display, scratching and clawing at each other like vicious felines.

"What on earth!" the Marquis of Ulster exclaimed.

They watched as the parents of the girls rushed forward, snatching at their daughters and forcibly removing them from the dance floor. Rowena saw Sheffield standing near them smiling broadly, as though he was watching some form of theatrical entertainment. When he noticed her watching, the smile disappeared from his lips. Yet even from across the room she could see the delight shining in his eyes.

As the girls and their families disappeared, a buzz of shocked whispers filled the room. Upset at what she'd seen, Rowena excused herself and finally made her way to the terrace. Walking to the low wall that curved around the edge of the veranda, she sat.

The scent of roses filled the air as she looked out over the garden. Her eyes traveled up over the treetops where she was delighted to find a clear, cloudless patch of dark sky above her, a crescent moon framed by the gathering clouds glowed in the distance with a single star dangling from its tip, like a diamond on velvet.

"The moonlight makes your face glow. I know you must be tired but sitting here you look happy and content."

Rowena rubbed her arms to warm them as she turned to watch de Grey step out of the shadows across the way.

"I shouldn't have come," she said. "I rarely enjoy these affairs and tonight-"

"I can take you home if you wish," Garret said, stepping closer.

"You needn't bother; I can manage on my own."

He stood silently watching her for a moment. "That was an unwarranted display in there a moment ago. Do you know the girls?"

"No, but Sheffield said they were part of the group he traveled with last year."

"Did you see him, the way he watched them? He appeared to be having a great laugh at their expense."

She stood and walked toward the ballroom door, searching for Sheffield in the crowd. She wouldn't admit it to Garret, but the look on Bradley's face during the catfight had upset her.

"He's been more interested in the darker side of people since we were children. I doubt he has any desire to change that now," she said.

"I think he's disgusting. You should be careful going about with him."

Rowena bit her lip. They'd had this

discussion before. "Garret, why don't you just leave me alone? I'm really in no mood for your company. I'll ask the doorman to call for my coach. Fagan will arrive soon."

"You've never forgiven me, have you?"

"Let the past be. Too many years have passed for us to dredge up those times."

"Then I'll leave you to find your way home. Rest well, my lady." He stopped and looked back at her. "Row, I believe you're right about that darkness falling over London. I think it will be a long time before the light returns."

Looking into his eyes, she saw a sincerity and sadness she'd missed before. She knew he wouldn't be pleased if she tried to interfere, yet of late he seemed different, more sincere. He still flaunted his indifference to his station in life. He still caroused with ruffians and men who appeared hardened by their experiences.

After leaving the main hall, it seemed only minutes before her coach arrived. The ride home was short. As she stepped out of the carriage a gust of damp wind whipped her cloak. Large, heavy drops of rain fell as a blinding flash streaked across the sky.

Stepping inside, she looked back as thunder cracked violently overhead, shaking the walls. A curtain of water fell where she had stood only a moment before. Instead of closing the door, she stood watching the storm, failing to recognize how brutal the nights were to become.

———

CHAPTER NINE

"Emma Smith died after a brutal attack. I don't know how she was able to walk to the common house. She was horribly injured, Lady Radcliffe." Dr. Hillier looked away from Rowena as he talked, trying to hide his disdain. "It was not something you should interest yourself in."

"She was one of my patients. I've been seeing her for several months. You know how vicious some of her...callers could become. She was often battered."

"Yes, well...I understand you've the blessing of the Duke to investigate such happenings, but I don't agree. I'll let you look at the report if you must, but I won't answer any more questions."

"Thank you doctor," she said as he quickly exited the office to gather the paperwork she had requested. *Damn these pompous old men, I'm a doctor and yet they treat me like some scabrous dog.*

Several long minutes later a nurse brought a folder and set it on the edge of the desk, sniffing her disapproval as she left.

As Rowena read the report, her heart sank. Although this was an attack by three men, she was certain one of them was the same one she had feared would arrive in London and begin to slaughter the prostitutes who walked the streets at night. It made no logical sense, but there was something...

Monday's *Morning Advertiser* carried the headlines "The Horrible Murder in Whitechapel." Little was left to the reader's imagination as it summarized the inquest.

> "*Mary Russell, the deputy keeper of a common lodging-house stated that the deceased left home on*

Monday evening in her usual health and returned between four and five next morning, suffering from horrible injuries. The woman told witnesses that she had been shockingly ill-treated by some men and robbed of her money."

The article continued describing the source of injury as a blunt object which had ruptured Emma Smith's peritoneum and other internal organs, causing her death. Rowena looked up as her housekeeper entered the room.

"Excuse me, my lady, you have a note from Lord Sheffield and his man is waiting for an answer."

"That's fine Margaret. Did you offer him some tea?"

"Yes mum, he be waitin' in the kitchen."

What does he want now?

Rowena read the note and wrote a reply, returning the paper to Margaret. "I'll be going to Sheffield's for tea, so you and cook can take a few hours off this afternoon."

Margaret smiled and curtsied before

117

rushing out of the room.

Rowena laughed quietly, knowing Margaret and Elizabeth would swiftly finish the morning chores so they could take time to stroll through some of their favorite shops. Four years ago the two women had met in the workhouse after their families had turned them out to fend for themselves. Margaret's mother had been ill, and unable to care for her children any longer, and the relatives had taken only the youngest of her siblings in to raise.

Elizabeth had arrived from the country in the company of a young man she believed had loved her, but when he reached London he'd pushed her out the door as soon as he discovered the life of gaming and drinking he had not experienced in their village. Ashamed, she had known she couldn't return home and had sought work. Both of the women had been lucky to have found jobs, as difficult and demoralizing as the work could be.

They had survived for a full year, until Rowena discovered them, sick and about to be thrown onto the streets again. She had them taken in and nursed them to health. When they had recovered, she'd sent them to be trained as domestics and been extremely pleased with the work they had done since. Glancing down at the newspaper, as she stood to dress to go the home of Bradley Sheffield, she thanked God the two young women had not been forced into the life so many of the women she met had accepted.

———

"Rowena, darling. I knew you'd come. You're such a good little girl, coming when called."

"You're being impertinent as usual, but then you said you were willing to help my charitable service. Surely you've not turned into a generous soul willing to offer hours of your time to help the poor."

"No, of course not, but you know of my servant Morgana Ridley, I wanted to offer *her* assistance."

"The companion who travels with you?"

"Yes. Yes, she is trained as a nurse and since I decided to stay here this year, I thought she might become bored."

"How noble of you. I don't suppose you've asked her if she is willing to do this."

"Why should I be bothered by what she is willing to do? After all, I am being quite *generous* to continue to pay her while she is in your hands."

Galt, Sheffield's butler, arrived with

the tray holding the tea and began to set it out, pouring a cup for each of them.

"Sheffield, you're outrageous." She sipped the tea. "Thank you Galt, I'm sure Lord Sheffield rarely tells you how much he appreciates your service to him."

"It is my duty, madam," the man said, giving a modest bow before leaving the room.

"So, when will you introduce me to Morgana?"

"She should be joining us shortly. Now, tell me about this murdered woman. I know you have every detail."

"Not really something I enjoy talking about over tea, and I'm sure you've read the reports in the papers."

"Yes, of course, but they don't describe all the wounds and all the injuries. Surely there is more than what I read."

Rowena studied him for several moments, not sure what she was seeing. It was almost the same look he'd had when he watched the girls fighting at the ball. Setting the cup on the table beside her, she stood and walked about the room. "Bradley, surely you don't find this woman's death an entertainment. What was done to her was tragic."

"Of course." He gave a small nod,

acknowledging her words. "You're correct, sorry if I gave you any other impression. I don't know what I was thinking." He walked over and placed his hand on her shoulder. "I forget this is not a game to you. Not the murder, but your involvement. Did you see the body? Of course you did, it must have been very difficult for you."

A knock interrupted them.

"Come," Sheffield called out, dropping his hand and turning to face the door. "Come in Morgana, this is Lady Radcliffe, Doctor Radcliffe. I told her you are interested in helping at her clinic since we won't be traveling this year."

Rowena studied the woman who stood with her hands clasped in front of her as though she was ready to pray. She peered back through dull dun-colored eyes, her mouse brown hair pulled back so tightly it appeared to stretch the skin of her rounded face. Her day dress had been washed until the color was completely leached from it.

"Thank you for the suggestion my Lord," she finally said in a thin, reedy voice. "The LORD sustains them on their sickbed; in their illness you heal all their infirmities. I shall be thankful to provide solace to those who seek your services, my lady."

"I don't preach to these women, Morgana, if that's what you have in mind."

"I am skilled as a nurse, having come from the house of Dr. Pederson after he passed to his reward. He encouraged me and trained me to assist him. Yet I've great faith in the word of the Lord."

Rowena hesitated. "Well, I'll be happy to have another pair of hands to assist if you wish to join me." Glancing at Sheffield, she wondered if his presence had forced the woman to volunteer. Was this something he thought would help him entertain himself in some way?

I've gotten to be suspicious of everything Bradley does. I must stop this. He may simply want to show some charity for a change.

"I'm happy Lord Sheffield is generous and will allow me the time to work with you. He is the kindest soul."

She would never call Bradley kind, but Morgana was certainly entitled to her opinion. "You can come with me tomorrow if you wish. I'm taking my day at the George Yard surgery and will be happy to have you there as well."

Matters were quickly settled and Morgana left the room as Bradley offered to have fresh tea provided. "Have you seen de Gray of late? I've heard he's running with the same rabble we saw him with at the inn several months ago. I'd think he'd be more careful of his friends. Such company could cause him to lose favor with those who count."

"I doubt he'd care much." Rowena set her cup aside. "He's never been one to worry overmuch about what anyone thinks of him. I think Albany finds that rather pleasurable in a somewhat perverse manner."

"Perhaps in the past." Sheffield lifted his eyebrow and seemed to puff up importantly. "But I have heard there are conversations behind closed doors against his arrogant ways."

"You listen too closely to the gossips. So what is this generous offer really about? You've never been known to do anything unless it benefits you personally. I have to admit this sudden display of charity rather astounds me. What are you seeking to gain from this little venture?"

"Rowena, you wound me," he pouted. "I'm trying for once to do something worthy of you. I've been so little help in your quests, I wanted to be sure I stay in your good graces."

123

Rowena couldn't hold back a chuckle. "Well, for the moment you are in my good books, even while you confirm my opinion you do only what pleases you."

Bradley Sheffield smiled like a cat intent on pouncing on a canary.

"Well, I must go." Rowena stood and collected her belongings. "I'll look forward to having Morgana attend the surgery. I'll send Fagan to collect her."

"Yes, good. I won't have to bother to find her transportation."

"Really, Bradley you make a generous offer then ruin it with your selfishness."

"Alright, I'll try to behave. You take care. I hear you roam those horrible streets at night. If there really is a killer, as you believe, you shouldn't be where he can mistake you for one of your unfortunates."

"You believe I could be in danger? That's a bit of a reach even for you."

"Perhaps, but heed my words. You are a beautiful woman and may attract unwarranted attention. Stay away from your charities after dark, Rowena. You're vulnerable. Awful things happen to people who walk the streets in the dark of night."

———

CHAPTER TEN

A young man burst through the door as Rowena was preparing to close the surgery and leave for the night. "Ya' got to come," he said, grabbing her arm in an attempt to pull her toward the door. "Quick Ben's been half murdered and needs ya'."

"Its okay, Fagan," she said to her driver who stood in the entrance door. "Go get the carriage."

"Pleeeez, we got ta' go," the boy said.

"Wait, I have to get my bag," she said pulling her arm from his hand and going back into the treatment room to retrieve it.

Rowena locked the surgery door. "Tell Fagan where we need to go, and then tell me what happened to Quick Ben."

"Ringers. Three dandies attacked him. He did nothin'. Was just standin' outside o' Ringers, barterin' with one of the doxies. No one was payin' no attention when they stroll down the street actin' so fine. Figured they was just out for a lark, check out us poor uns, liken they do. Then the smallest one just stuck a knife in 'im."

"Did O'Hara call the police?'

"Wha' for? Police do nuthin' for the likes o' us.'

"It needs to be reported. Fagan will help you find a constable when we get there, and you tell them I want them to come make a report."

The carriage pulled up in front of the pub, and the small crowd parted to allow Rowena access to Quick Ben who lay on the ground, snarling and cursing at anyone who tried to help. The man was lucky. If the knife had been just an inch to the left of where it still protruded from his chest, Ben would have been dead by the time Rowena had arrived.

"Quick Ben, I am Dr. Radcliffe. O'Hara sent for me and I intend to remove that knife and care for the wound. If you are going to fight me, I will have some of these men hold you down," she said as she set her bag on the ground, opening it.

"O 'ara?" The fight went out of him and he lay watching her closely as she selected the items she needed.

Rowena sliced open his shirt before removing the knife, as she mentally reviewed the placement of organs and muscle tissue in the area it had penetrated. Convinced by Ben's demeanor and color, she felt sure the blade had damaged only muscle. She cleaned the skin about the cut, and then withdrew the dagger from his chest, placing clean sponges into the wound to staunch the bleeding.

"Damn woman, have a care," he swore his face turning pale as she removed the knife. "Ya tryin' ta kill me since those dandies didn't do the job?"

"I know it hurt and it may be worse when I sew this wound closed," she said. "It will hurt. I could use medication to make you sleep while I work on you, but I would prefer not to with you here on the street."

"Naw, just give me Irish whiskey 'n I'll be dandy. You just do what ya' got ta' do."

Shouts sounded from the crowd

and several of the men took off running. The gawkers left standing about parted to watch the chase, which allowed Rowena to see three finely dressed men under the light a block away, laughing as they turned to run away in the opposite direction. She couldn't see them clearly, but something about them looked familiar. She might have been tempted to investigate if she hadn't needed to tend to the man lying on the ground beside her.

Carefully she cleaned out the wound and stitched the gaping flesh together; covering it with the salve she carried before placing a bandage over it. "Quick Ben, I need to be sure you are listening," she said as she moved the whiskey bottle out of his hand, setting it aside. "You must keep this clean, I have soap and salve for you to use. In two days, take this bandage off, wash the stitched area and put the salve on it, then re-bandage. Do this for the next six days. If the edges of the cut become puffy and red or appears to be infected, you must come to the surgery."

"Don' need such a fuss over a little knifin'," Quick Ben said.

"But you are going to do as I say? Or will I have to have O'Hara repeat my instructions?"

"Naw, I do whats you tell me."

Satisfied Rowena packed up her supplies, finishing just as the gang who had chased the boys returned, cursing their lack of luck in capturing them. Moments later Fagan and the PC rounded the corner.

Quick Ben and the witnesses told the constable what had happened, and about the chase.

"I think I saw the carriage those ruffians must have come in when I was searching for the constable, my lady," Fagan said. "It was a phaeton, but I couldn't see who was driving and it was too dark to see the colors. Don't know who it might belong to."

A small carriage carrying Abberline and de Grey pulled to the curb. "What are you doing here at this time of night without proper protection?" de Grey growled. "Woman, do you not understand these streets are dangerous?

Garret was too close and Rowena took a step back. "I have Fagan to watch out for me, "she said as she started to turn away.

"Row, the constable reported Fagan was with him, which means he wasn't with

129

you. I'm not going to have-"

"What? What are you not going to have? You have no reason to worry about me and no authority over me. Garrett, you have no business telling me what to do. Now step away, we don't need to have a spat in the streets."

Abberline finished talking with the victim and those witnesses who would provide information. "Looks like some young dandies were out for a bit of sport. Unfortunately they appear to have taken things too far. Not sure we will be able to do much about it though, unless they go on the prowl again and one of the PC's spots them. The witnesses couldn't tell us much more than that they were wearing fancy clothes and top hats."

"I think they were down the street while I was treating Quick Ben," Rowena said. "There was something familiar but I couldn't really see their faces under the light. Fagan says he may have seen their carriage but he won't be able to identify it either."

Biting her lip, she wondered if this might be the beginning. Young men of stature randomly attacking people on the streets were a common theme in the towns

where the other women had been viciously
slain. Surely it wasn't just a coincidence.

———

CHAPTER ELEVEN

Rowena spent the days working in the surgery. Marchioness Ulster had been true to her word, and sent an invitation to tea so they could talk of the work Rowena was doing. She smiled as Doctor Lucinda Patterson came into the room to relieve her for the afternoon.

"It has been a busy day. Morgana's been a godsend, though she does carry the bible with her when she has the chance."

"She's very helpful, but a bit dour."

"Well, we accept what we can when it comes to help. I'm feeling a bit guilty. I seem to be gone quite a lot lately. However, it's vital we continue to gather support for our activities." She handed Lucinda a small purse containing the coins to be distributed among those who'd seek their medical services and quickly returned home to bathe and change into more appropriate clothes for the visit.

She arrived at the Marchioness' home on time and was escorted out to the gardens where tea had already been set and the Marchioness sat with several of her friends.

"Rowena, I am so glad you could join us. You know Lady Kennington and Lady Highsmythe?"

Rowena acknowledge each of the women before taking the seat the Marchioness indicated.

"We've heard so many amazing stories about your work," Lady Highsmythe said, setting her tea cup aside and reaching for a sugar biscuit. "I think it would be exciting to be of some assistance, but I've no skills to assist you."

Rowena smiled. "There's other work to be done, not only treating the illnesses."

"And what would you suggest?" Lady Kennington asked.

"Schools to train young women who

have been abandoned to this sad fate could be established. They can be taught the skills to work in places like your own home or a shop. I myself have two such women I was able to help leave the workhouses. Not only are they excellent in keeping my house and kitchens, they are loyal, happy and healthy."

"What an unusual suggestion," Lady Ulster lowered her tea cup into her lap.

"As you know, I am considered quite an unusual person." Rowena laughed. She was pleased these women seemed to genuinely care and wish to do something for others. "There are so many who have needs and have been forgotten.

"I'm not suggesting those who work on the streets be taken in and trained. Unfortunately, most of them have gone beyond our ability to change their ways, but there are many young women forced to work in slavish conditions. Some of them actually sleep on the street and are in constant danger from ruffians. Many have been abandoned by their families because they're too expensive to feed any longer. It's a sad thing."

"I've heard you've personally sent many women on to be trained as nurses and even a few to the medical schools that now accept women, is this true?"

"It always amazes me how much we know of each others' private affairs." Rowena smiled and glanced at the faces of the three women. "Yes, Lady Kennington, I've done this and will continue. It would be wonderful if you wish to help in this endeavor."

The Marchioness glanced at Rowena and pursed her lips. "I've heard so many rumors about you, do you mind if I ask what made you decide to become a doctor? Is it true you have worked with villains in the prisons in America?"

"And did you really attend the ball with Bradley Sheffield?" Millicent Highsmythe piped in. "I have heard the wicked things about him. Are they true?"

Rowena tried to keep from choking on the tea she sipped. "It seems you know much of my business. I suppose the rumor mill is very healthy these days. I'd forgotten how efficient the gossips are at collecting and passing along their tales."

"Oh, dear, I offended you," Lady Highsmythe said, frowning. I didn't mean to. I just love a wicked story, you know."

"Yes, I was with Bradley, though I left before he did."

Lady Ulster gave tolerant smile. "I

am sorry my dear, but I have little control over my good friend."

Rowena laughed. "I must admit I didn't know Bradley would cause such talk. He is rather wicked, but I have never found him to be less than a gentleman when I am with him."

"Well, I heard the most shocking tales of when he traveled with those children. Wasn't it just horrifying how those girls got into that uncomely fight? I hear they are very wicked and your Bradley Sheffield has helped to make them that way. Reggie, my dear husband, says it is rumored he carried those children to some of the darkest parts of the cities they visited," Millicent assured them.

"I'm not sure I understand," Rowena said, though she was afraid she understood too well.

"Well, Reggie says James Betterfield's son, Manfred, saw them touring the...oh, dear how should I say it?"

"Millicent, just say it and stop dithering. You've never been one to guard your words before today," Lady Ulster snapped. "Get on with it or hush. This is not the reason I have Lady Radcliffe present."

"Well, I head he took them to

several of those houses of ill repute in France. Not only the boys, I mean a man must learn of the world, but he had the *girls* with him as well."

Rowena sat back, stunned. Surely not. Sheffield was odd, outrageous, but he could never do such a thing. Could he?

"Millicent, you can't believe such drivel," Marchioness Ulster exclaimed. "The Betterfield boy must have made it up. He's always been one to seek out attention."

"Well, Reggie believes it," Lucinda said as she sat back, her lips drawn into a pout. "You can think what you want."

Marchioness Ulster turned to face Rowena. "Never mind my friend. She is addle pated and would believe the sky was orange should her Reggie tell her so. So my dear, I asked you why you decided on this unusual vocation."

Rowena understood Lady Ulster had no desire to continue to speculate on the behavior of Bradley Sheffield, nor did she, but the sinking feeling in the pit of her stomach made it difficult to focus on the matters the marchioness wished to discuss. She inhaled deeply, concentrating before answering. "I found the men of the medical profession to be highly offensive.

When my mother became ill they ignored my questions and treated me as a pesky dog or cat that was in their way."

"I knew you mother, she was a gentle and loving soul. Many admired her."

"Thank you. I remember that about her as well. She was one to encourage me to follow my heart."

"You were young when she passed away. Perhaps you were being protected and not ignored."

"I was eighteen, not young in these times. No, they ignored me because I was a woman and they ignored my mother's wishes because she was ill. They believed they were superior in every way. Even the little requests she made were scoffed at when they believed her asleep. It hurt her deeply. I'll never forgive them for their attitudes."

"So you have something to prove?" Lady Highsmythe asked gently.

"I needed to understand what happened. It took training to learn about her condition. Unfortunately, even today there's nothing we could have done to save her. However, I believe there are things those men shouldn't have done, and I'll try my best to assure similar treatments are never given to my patients, nor those who are treated by the women I've had trained."

"You're turning the medical world around here topsy-turvy." Lady Kennington giggled and bit her lip, an expression that seemed to indicate she felt wicked using such a term. "I've been told you're planning on opening your own school. I imagine these stuffed shirts are quite aggrieved."

"Millicent!" Lady Ulster gasped. "I can't believe those words came out of your mouth." She covered her mouth with her napkin, but Rowena noted her eyes crinkled as she grinned.

"I've been attended by such men on occasion and found them most unpleasant and snobbish. Besides, I believe we came to your home to speak our minds." Lady Kennington bounced in her chair as if to give more weight to her words, an expression of pleasure glowing on her face.

"Yes, well." Lady Ulster flushed and briefly looked uncomfortable. "Lady Radcliffe, I wanted to hear of your adventures with these horrible villains. Is it true you actually worked with killers and thieves?"

Rowena didn't try to repress the smile on her face. "Yes, my lady, I did indeed. It was most fascinating. As part of my training I was required to work in several settings and the prison was the one I found most interesting."

Lady Highsmythe gasped. "I would have fainted if I'd had to look at such a person. I'm shocked you were able to do so."

"I assure you fainting is not something you'd wish to do in front of those men. You must present a very careful appearance of being in charge. They'll try to make you believe they have the upper hand at any sign of weakness." Rowena remembered well the way the worst had acted on their first meeting.

"I'd think with your upbringing you could quell them into submission," the Marchioness said.

"I believe it helped, but the very atmosphere in the prison is enough to make you doubt who you are and what you know. However, once I adjusted I found I was intrigued to understand the workings of their minds."

"They must be insane. That's the only answer," Lady Kennington said.

"But they aren't. Many of them seem to be quite ordinary until you begin to question their reasons for killing and how they manage to overcome the horror of their actions."

"Ordinary? How can that be?"

"I assure you Lady Kennington, their appearance and even their demeanor would not attract your attention if you met them on the street while taking a stroll. No, it's not something you see when you meet them, rather it's the way their minds work, and none of us have the ability to read what another is thinking."

"You only say that to frighten us," Kennington snapped.

"Hillary, you're being rude. Lady Radcliffe is only answering our questions. Go on my dear, I find this intriguing."

"Thank you." Rowena gave a light laugh. "I don't wish to give you nightmares, but I find I have a deep interest in the minds of these types of men. As I said, they can appear very normal and even polite, but they have something missing. They don't seem to have emotions as others do, and they find nothing wrong with the actions they have taken."

"I had no idea all those men they keep in prison were so fearsome." Lady Highsmythe shivered, her eyes round as an owls as she listened intently.

"I'm speaking of only a few of the men I examined. Many in the prisons are

141

saddened by what they did in their past or angry because they feel the victim forced them into the situation which caused their imprisonment. The few I speak of are very different and do not display the sadness or the anger of the others."

Lady Highsmythe glanced at her pocket watch. "I apologize, but I must leave soon. I promised my husband I'd be available when his new horse arrived this afternoon. He's building his racing stables and is as excited as a child over this new addition. I admit I have found all of this fascinating."

Rowena expressed her thanks for the interest the women had displayed, gathered her belongings and rose to leave, suddenly feeling neglectful. She hadn't told them death was coming.

———

She stepped out of the house to find Bradley Sheffield leaning against a lamp post. She felt uneasy, after the gossip she'd just heard, but surely there was no truth to the matter. Yet she had no desire to deal with him at his moment.

"Bradley, *what* are you doing here?" Rowena glanced toward her carriage, suddenly wishing she could just run to it and get in.

"I was out, and saw your conveyance, as I was just returning from some mundane chores. I thought I'd take a chance and hope you'd be finished chatting with your lady friends."

"So you sent your own carriage off?" This was just a bit too presumptuous. Surely he didn't expect her to offer him transportation to his home or to another destination.

"Oh, it'll be back soon, if you are saying you don't wish my company."

"It's...I..."

"Row. Isn't that what de Grey used to call you? I thought we were great friends. Has something changed? I was sure you'd find this a pleasurable surprise."

She carefully maintained a neutral face, while internally she felt her stomach twist. Was it disgust? Fear? She couldn't put her finger on it. "Of course not, I just didn't expect to see you. I had other things on my mind as I came through the door."

"Wonderful, then we'll slip down and have a stroll though Hyde Park or Regent's if you prefer. It's early and there's really nothing else to do."

"Bradley, I really have some things-"

"What could be more important than

a few hours of talk with a good friend? You don't want me to feel I've been rejected, do you?" He walked over and took her arm, leaning in toward her when she would have stepped back out of his way.

Damnation.

Sometimes she really hated that society demanded she be polite. Sheffield just didn't seem to understand there were certain boundaries, even in friendship. Nor, it occurred to her, did he even really seem to care. "I don't wish to be rude, but I really have other business to care for. If you wish to go for a ride in the park, perhaps you can find a more suitable companion."

She thought she saw anger flare in his eyes, but it was gone so quickly she couldn't be sure.

"Yes, of course. I should have left a card earlier, or called you on the phone this morning. I feel like you're trying to avoid me, even though I can think of nothing I've done to offend."

He watched her as though trying to read her thoughts and it made her even more uncomfortable. Thankfully, his carriage turned the corner just as she was wondering what to do next. It would have been almost impossible to leave him just standing on the street in front if the Ulster home.

"I am sorry Sheffield. We will have to take the stroll some other time. I have an appointment I cannot alter."

He watched her climb into her carriage and remained standing at the curb until Fagan had driven away. She'd seen the look he gave her as they passed him, and for just a moment she felt fear. She had seen the same look on the face of the men she had interviewed, the men she had just been discussing.

———

CHAPTER TWELVE

"Is the truth mum, Bitty just fell over, dead as a duck there in front of the bloke. They was jus' walkin' down the street."

"I am so sorry, Catherine. I have a hard time believing it. She was young and I just saw her a week ago, I believe. I think Morgana helped put a dressing on the burn she had, but she looked to be in good health." Rowena wrapped the bandages around the woman's arm where she'd covered a sore with her salve.

"Yeah, she seen that Morgana. A right bible quoter she is. Bitty said she tole her she was goin' to 'ell. Got a good laugh out of it, she did." Catherine's smile exposed her blackened teeth.

Rowena glanced across the room where Morgana stood winding bandages and listening to the conversation. Although her back was turned Rowena was sure she was muttering her prayers in the presence of the "unclean."

I'll have to talk to her. I cannot have her preaching to these women, they'll stop coming for help. Her attitude toward them shows too easily.

"These been sad days, Lady Doctor. First old Emma getting' done in months back. Last month Pipin' Penny just up and died while she was...well it would na be proper for me to say to your face. Now Bitty. Seems like we be losin' one or two of me friends ever week."

Rowena nodded her agreement, wondering about the coincidence. So many of the women who'd died recently had been tended at the surgery shortly before their deaths. *Odd.* But what could it mean? There were so many women on the streets, in the factories and workhouses. Yes, it was unusual so many of the women who had been her patients seemed to have died, but the life they led could easily explain it. Mentally giving herself a shake, she handed Catherine the standard pot of salve and a few coins.

"I know." Catherine laughed before Rowena could speak. "Keep it clean and use the paste regular."

As Catherine closed the door behind her, Morgana directed an evil-looking smile at Rowena. "The Lord is smiting the unclean."

"Morgana, I won't have you talking that way in the surgery. I have spoken to you about this before. These women need our help and our generosity. They do not need to hear what sinners they are. There are any number of men and women who taunt them daily as well as ardent ministers who track them down."

"I'm bound to dispense the word of God," Morgana declared. "I cannot choose the place, only the opportunity. Leviticus 5:2 *when any of you touch any unclean thing—whether the carcass of an unclean beast or the carcass of unclean livestock or the carcass of an unclean swarming thing—and are unaware of it, you have become unclean, and are guilty.* I weep for your soul as well my lady."

Rowena chose to ignore this. She'd already spoken to Morgana several times in regard to her duties to help these unfortunate women. Sighing deeply, she decided she would have to speak with Sheffield, see if he could add his influence. If not it was possible she would have to forgo Morgana's able assistance.

A disturbance in the other room drew her from her thoughts. Believing a disagreement between the women waiting there was beginning, she rushed to intercede. Opening the door she found Minnie Trotter lying on the floor violently ill, the others huddled into a corner as far away as they could get. "Morgana, I need your assistance. Now," she called sharply. "What happened?" she asked the women across the room.

"Doan know mum, she was talking to us and jus' fell over. She looked a bit peaked and maybe drunk, you know," Annie said, the others nodding their agreement.

Rowena stooped down and quickly examined the young woman, noting a sheen of moisture, and the trembling of her body. Laying her hand on the woman's face she found it cold and clammy. There was no odor of ale or other form of drink.

"Let me, Lady Radcliffe," Morgana said as she scooped the small woman into her arms.

Rowena watched in disbelief as Morgana rose and carried the woman to the table in the examination room. Minnie was not large but was limp from the illness and must weigh at least four or five stone.

Together the women worked over the young woman. Morgana cleaned her face and helped her take laudanum to calm her stomach as Rowena recommended. She could only hope this was just a bout of gastric fever.

Nothing eased Minnie's pain. The trembling worsened and Rowena noted a yellowish tint to her skin as a spasm gripped the young woman. She quickly went to the reference books she kept on the shelves of the room, trying to determine some other course of action to stop the worsening symptoms, but could find nothing that helped.

As Morgana continued to watch over their patient, Rowena went out to talk to the others who were waiting their turn. "Mary, I want you to find a constable and have him call for an ambulance. I need to send Minnie to the hospital and neither I nor Nurse can leave her. Annie, you and the others should come back tomorrow. I'm sorry, but until Minnie is delivered to the ambulance, we will have to continue to help her as much as we can. If you wish to stay, you may wait in the front room until I can see you."

The women moved into the tiny waiting room. Although they could not all be termed friends to each other, they lived in a community where violence and even death were accepted though feared. Rowena knew they were expecting the worst. She did as well.

Returning to the treatment room she found Morgana cleaning the woman, who had soiled herself. Soon the ambulance arrived and Minnie was delivered to the men who moved her into the cart unhurriedly, driving off with instructions to have the doctor at the hospital contact Rowena at her home if they needed any additional information.

The women who had been waiting had various reactions as they watched Minnie being carried out of the surgery, but Rowena recognized these as fear. Fear that the girl would die. Fear for their own mortality. Fear because they did not know what was happening.

Most of the woman followed the young woman to the waiting conveyance, then left while a few others, spoke quietly before leaving, to discouraged to stay for treatment.

As she prepared to leave, she saw the smirk on Morgana's lips but didn't encourage the woman to speak. *She thinks these unfortunate women deserve to be punished.* Setting the thought aside, she finished collecting her things, briefly thanked the woman for her assistance, and directed her to go home.

As she walked into the town house, the jangling of the new phone jarred her. Margaret quickly answered and informed her Lord Sheffield wished to speak with her.

"Tell him I will call back later," she said as she walked past the device and up the stairs.

I really don't want to talk to him right now.

"I want to freshen up. It's been a hard day. After you give him my message, I'd also appreciate a strong cup of tea."

"Yes, my lady." Margaret delivered the message to the caller, then set the phone in its cradle and went to prepare the requested refreshment.

"My Lady," Margaret said as she carried the tray to a small table beside the chair where Rowena sat. "I've a note for you from Lord de Grey, his man delivered it just as I was coming up." Taking the letter from her pocket she handed it to Rowena and went to prepare a warm bath. "I'll put some lavender in to sooth perhaps you can spend a quiet evening. You appeared to be troubled."

Rowena smiled weakly. "Yes, I am. I fear one of my patients is very ill and may not recover. I sent her on to hospital but fear they won't be able to do more than I. Sad, she is a young woman, one I had hoped to help move off the streets."

"I can never show you how grateful I am for the assistance you gave me. Elizabeth and I both know how fortunate we are to have had your care and concern. God bless you, and don't blame yourself, you *can't* save everyone."

"Your words help," Rowena said as she opened the envelope quickly reading the message. "It looks like I'll have to forgo the quiet evening. I had forgotten I'd promised to meet Lord de Grey and his missive has been a gentle reminder of the fact. I'll be dining out this evening, so let Elizabeth know she'll be cooking only for you and the household staff."

———

The dining room patrons spoke quietly, a low hum filling the room as they were escorted to their table. The flickering candles set in the center of each table caused the crystal to sparkle. The aroma of the dishes already served to others floated though the air. de Grey quickly ordered wine. The sommelier brought it and prepared it for tasting. A second waiter took their order then dropped the curtains to their private space.

"I saw Swanson today. We had a lively discussion about you and your interest in murder," de Grey explained. "He finds you quite interesting and would like to meet one day just to talk about your theories on these matters."

"Why did he tell you? He could have called or sent an invitation."

"First, I believe he is too aware of your rank and your connections. He, by comparison, has more humble beginnings. I also believe he finds you quite beautiful and as he is unmarried, perhaps he thinks it would be better if he has an intermediary."

Her laughter bubbled out. "I find it fascinating he would have you as his agent. Then perhaps he doesn't realize we're not close. The only time we both met him was at the CID offices and you were most civil there."

"Rowena, we were friends for many years before we became merely acquaintances. Can't we put our differences aside? I don't remember what caused this riff, and I've always respected you, believed in your abilities and found you to be highly intelligent. Are these not the qualities you wish to have people admire?"

Sitting back she studied his face for several minutes. His dark eyes were sincere. "Yes, those are the things most important to me, and I don't want to remember either," she said as her heart twisted remembering how hurt she had been to find him gone. She had loved him. Believed they would always be together. Then he had just disappeared. It felt as though her heart had been torn into small pieces. The pain had almost been unbearable.

He had been drifting away from her and they had fought. Fought about the dangerous looking men he suddenly seemed unable to live without. Fought about the way he would suddenly disappear for days at a time. Fought about the secrecy and the lies he told. The last

155

night she had seen him had been the worst fight they'd had. Yet she had believed he would still be there for her, Believed somehow they would be able to make it right.

"Row?"

"Sorry." To avoid looking into his eyes she looked at the table. Straightened the silver. Fussed with the napkin. "If we are to become friends once more, you must tell me why I find you in places I would not expect you to be."

De Grey smiled, "Well, it's somewhat difficult to explain. Perhaps we should speak of less serious matters? I hear there's a new play everyone is raving about. Perhaps you'd like to join me one evening for some entertainment."

Rowena's eyes flashed. "I see, you respect me and find me intelligent, but don't want to speak on serious subjects. You've been a rogue most of your life. You keep the company of the rowdiest kind of men. And you still seem intent on keeping secrets. What are you up to Storm?"

"Unfortunately I'm not free to answer the question. I will however tell you I believe you're correct in your suspicions the men who have been punished for crimes in Newcastle and Germany are not those who committed the atrocities. I also believe your senses are correct, and the person you seek is here, in London. I don't know, however, why things are so quiet. The woman in Oxford was murdered in February. Here it is almost the end of July and there...have been no further discoveries of similar events. Though you suspected one woman died at the hand of this killer."

"Are you working for the Home Office perhaps? Otherwise, what concern are these matters to you?"

Rather than answering, he refilled her wine glass, and beckoned the waiter to bring the soup course.

"So you won't answer. I find that telling in itself. If this is the game you wish to play... So when do you wish me to meet with you and Chief Inspector Swanson? I'll have to make arrangements if you want to luncheon, to have one of the other doctors present at the surgery."

De Grey gave her several dates, and when they agreed on one, he changed the subject. "I understand you have a new assistant, that Ridley woman, Bradley's supposed nurse. She and those children Sheffield dragged around last year were quite an astonishing sight."

The soup course finished, the waiter silently slipped the next course in front of them.

Garrett continued, "Don't you find her somewhat over enthusiastic in her devotions to Sheffield? She hovers over him in an unnatural manner. I find her disturbing. I met her when they were in Germany and she talked as though she needed to save everyone's soul. Her words were not reflected in her eyes, which are hard and hate filled."

"She is somewhat overzealous, but she is well trained in the field of medical service," Rowena said taking a small bite of lamb. "I admit, though, I'm considering trying to get Bradley to speak with her about her constant preaching. She ignores my admonitions to hold her tongue and I can't seem to make her understand my surgery is not the place for her to expound on her beliefs."

"I'm surprised you need him to intercede. You've never had trouble getting your servants to do as told in the past."

"I have the feeling she believes she need not take note of what I say, since she is actually employed by Bradley."

Garrett took a sip of wine, taking a

moment to consider what she had said. "Well, he'll discourage her if he thinks it's important to you. You can be assured the behavior will stop should he ask. I don't think he realizes she adores him. You know he has tight control over her and she would do anything he might ask."

"It's a strange relationship to be sure. I was surprised he offered to continue to employ her and allow her to come assist me. He is not normally a charitable man."

"It is strange. I wonder what he's up to. Is he planning to travel? It seems late for him to be leaving unless he plans to go south later this year. I haven't heard him mention any preparations."

"He claims not, although I don't understand why he would be content to stay here. Most of the people he spends time with have already left or will soon leave the city."

As they continued their conversation, courses were eaten and removed. "I find I've enjoyed your company this evening, Garret. I believe I've missed you some," she said as she stood and collected her purse and gloves, ready to leave the restaurant.

"Missed me, Rowena? I didn't think

I would ever hear those words from your lips.

What had she done? She didn't want him to think she cared, then a slip of the tongue and of course he'd caught it. "Garret, I have missed the man you once were. I admit I have missed him very much, but please don't read anything into my words. I know we can never go back to what we had been."

Garret stared at her for several seconds and she was afraid he would know she was lying. She did miss him, the man of the past and the man of the present. She wished she could change the way things were, but it was impossible. Wasn't it?

Garret smiled. "Perhaps I was reading too much into your words. For now let us just be friendly acquaintances and you can allow me the joy of escorting you for a turn in the park. I came in the Barouche and can have my driver lower the top; it's a rather pleasant evening."

First Bradley, now Garret, what was this sudden fascination with driving though a park?

"No, I'm tired. It was a difficult day, and just before I left to join you here I had word one of the women I cared for had died."

"I know that wounds you, I'm sorry. Was she badly hurt?" he asked as he helped her into the carriage.

"What? No she wasn't beaten or anything, she appeared to have gastric fever, but that's very unusual on one so young. The way she looked, I almost wondered if she had eaten something or...I don't know. She reminded me of a patient I had while I was in training. One who had been poisoned by his wife. She used something he purchased to kill rats. I know there are many pests in the East End, but I don't think people there spend their meager wages on poisons to eliminate them."

———

CHAPTER THIRTEEN

"I don't like it. Rowena has more sense than this. I can't believe she's friendly with Sheffield. The man is dangerous."

"Calm down de Grey. Sheffield would never hurt her. He wants her I think, almost enough to subdue his true nature." Albany sipped his whiskey as he watched Garret pace. "What did you learn today?"

"Nothing. I know he has something to do with the death of that woman back in April, Emma Smith. The attack bore many similarities to the ones in Germany and France. He and that pack of bloody little gentlemen and women, along with that *woman* he touts as a nurse, were in every one of the cities when the attacks occurred."

"You can suspect him of misdeeds all you want, but you have no proof, and I wonder you've grown so agitated. Perhaps it's more about Rowena than Lord Sheffield."

"Enough. I don't care what Rowena does or doesn't do, as long as she stays safe. It's difficult to watch her running all over the place every time she pleases; ignoring the danger she places herself in. I've had to add another man to the task of protecting her. She is much too observant for her own good and notices my men when they follow for too long.

I had Finnegan following her and she strode right up to him on the street, asking him if he planned to cut her purse. She has no sense, acting in such a manner. She's lucky it wasn't one of the lunatics who infest the streets."

"Perhaps he was not as invisible as you gave him credit for. She is observant. Occasionally I change the way I sit my hat, or carry a watch she has never seen and she always notices. It's one of the reasons I want to have her at the site when these attacks begin. If they begin, as you believe they will. I admit I am growing tired of waiting."

"I can't believe you gave her your blessing."

"Sit down de Grey, have a drink. I'll even pour if you will just stop wearing the stones to dust."

"Sorry, I know I shouldn't be so upset, but if you'd heard her over lunch, talking about murderers and mutilation with Swanson. She even had theories about the types of men who commit these horrors. Believes they're not insane. Bloody hell. The worst of it was Donald shared many of her views."

"You would rather she was the kind of woman who talks of petit point or the latest dance? Would you find her so fascinating if she giggled behind her fan?"

"I don't find her *fascinating*. She's difficult and-"

"I've known you since you were a lad, don't try to dismiss me or fool yourself. You've long found her far more attractive than any other woman. So tell me of these theories."

"She actually believes you can create categories for different types of killers. Men who seek power and those

164

who believe they have a mission. She suggested there may be other types as well, and she has a list of behaviors she says determine which type of killer they are. It could be intriguing if it weren't so ludicrous. As I said, even Chief Inspector Swanson seemed to agree to some of what she said."

"You say these theories are absurd but perhaps they have some merit."

"If you'd been there you'd probably have fallen under her spell and come away an advocate. I think you want her to be right about everything she's told you."

"So you believe the men who were hanged in Newcastle and Oxford were the killers and she is chasing a phantom?"

Garret set his drink down and scrubbed his hands over his face. "No, I think she's correct about those men, she has a sense...of evil, I'd say. I've never seen anyone so able to detect what's in another man's soul. When we were young, she kept me from making horrid mistakes. That's another thing, she can make you believe."

"Well, my friend, I charge you with assuring her safety. If you're correct, there's someone who will mark our streets with blood. I don't want them to have the slightest opportunity of causing her harm. You're sure your men can be trusted to take care and guard her well?"

"They're extremely capable and strong. No harm will come to her as we watch, but I can't promise he'll not reach her. Not in the sense he could touch her, but I fear what she'll see will burn into her soul."

———

As was usual, it was raining as Rowena arrived at the surgery. Opening the door to the treatment room, Rowena could hear Morgana chastising a group of women she appeared to have trapped in the corner. Their eyes were heated and they cringed when she flung her hand toward them, but none of them tried to escape the tirade until she entered the room.

Morgana's voice rose in fervor as she admonished her captive audience, "*If you sow to your own flesh, you will reap corruption from the flesh; but if you sow to the Spirit, you will reap eternal life from the Spirit.*

"*Morgana.* What do you think you're doing?" Anger sliced through Rowena like a knife. "Leave them alone. I have told you I will not tolerate this behavior. I want you to collect your things and leave immediately. You're no longer welcome here."

Morgana hissed, "The lord will strike you down, just as he has the unclean."

"Fagan," Rowena called to her driver, "escort this woman *out*. Take her to Lord Sheffield's. Advise him I'll call later. I want them both to understand she is *never* to return here." She felt her skin crawl as the woman turned feverish eyes on her and smiled evilly.

Fagan escorted Morgana from the room and stuffed her into the carriage before taking his place behind the horses, driving away.

Doctor Patterson, who had been taking a shift was standing in the doorway of the examination room, face reddened as she admitted she had been unable to control the nurse. "I told her to stop, I don't know what happened. Suddenly this afternoon, she began to rant at every one of the women who came in. I did ask her to leave but she just ignored me."

"It's not your fault. I've noticed she seemed less able to control her ravings of late. Since Minnie was so ill and died, she seems to have changed. Muttering bible quotations under her breath while she cleaned, encouraging me to use my influence to strengthen the laws against prostitution. Perhaps her religious zeal and working here has just grown too much for her."

"It seems such a shame. She was good when assisting in almost every situation." Lucinda closed the door between the exam room and the outer area. "She was well trained by her former employer."

"Yes, well I'll talk to Lord Sheffield. Perhaps he can find her a situation where she's not confronted every day by those she believes are such an abomination. When I first brought her in, she appeared so dedicated. I wonder what happened to change that."

"It can be difficult to work with some of these women every day," Lucinda admitted, and I find myself wanting to counsel them on their lives. But you are right, there are enough who want to work on their souls and the women would not come as often, even for the pittance we provide them, if they were made to feel uncomfortable."

"You're a warm and generous woman, Lucinda, and an excellent doctor." Rowena went to remove her cloak. "I'll stay and assist you since I caused you the inconvenience."

"No, really, I can take care of the rest of our ladies. There are only a few and I've already given them a cursory look. None of them will require much help. Really, I can attend them myself."

When Fagan returned with her coach, she directed him to take her home, where she went directly to the morning room and sat at her desk. After a moment's consideration she penned a brief note and invited Sheffield to her home for dinner. Not waiting for his reply, she directed Elizabeth on the dishes she wanted prepared.

At the time designated, she heard Lord Sheffield's carriage draw up in front of the house. Taking her time, she finished preparations before descending the stairs and joining him in the drawing room. "Sheffield. I wasn't sure you would be available."

"Somehow I doubt that statement. You know full well I'll come to you any time you so much as crook a finger, Rowena. You indicated in your note you needed my advice."

"I'm sure by now you're aware of

what happened this afternoon. I dismissed Morgana and told her not to return. She's become quite difficult and I'm concerned for her welfare. It surprises me to know you have such a person in your home."

His slow smile sought to be gracious, but failed to melt the chill in his eyes. She took note of the way the vein in his neck pulsed. In anger?

"I have had the benefit of Morgana's rendition of these matters. I suppose you're going to give me maudlin little details."

"No. Of course not. I was angry this afternoon. I've talked with her on several occasions about her behavior toward the women I attend. However, I don't want you to treat her harshly. Perhaps there's another position you can lend her to that will better suit her...beliefs."

"Surely this little discussion is not the full reason you had me call upon you."

"I invited you to dinner because I have been neglecting my duties in that area. I did so tonight because I wanted to assure myself that you'll not over react to the situation. Bradley I have seen you when you're embarrassed or upset, you can be difficult."

"You mean cruel, however that's not

the case here. I understand Morgana. Though the religious platitudes she spouts are boring at best, I find her interesting in ways that you would not understand. The entertainment she provides me is one of the reasons I'm determined not to lose her to another house. When I decide to go abroad again, she can be most useful if I decide to have anyone accompany me."

"I certainly don't understand your fascination, but I've never completely understood you."

"My sources tell me you lunched with de Grey. What's that about? I thought you detested him. Meeting at the Savin Trace was very daring of you. I understand their private rooms are not always used for eating."

"Your sources of information are impeccable as always, but there was no dallying behind the curtains. It was an afternoon of coming to terms. I believe we'll be more civil from this point, but does it matter? You've always hated him and I don't know why. What I do or do not have to do with him won't change your feelings toward each other."

The butler, Günter, announced dinner. She allowed Sheffield to escort her to the dining room, but found herself revolted by his touch. When the soup had been served the discussion continued.

"I don't trust him, Rowena. I remember a time when you talked of evil in those around you and believe he's a danger to you. Take care."

"I have no sense of harm from him. You Bradley have a much darker soul, yet I'm still your friend."

He stared at her for several minutes before he changed the subject. The way his look bore into her made her uncomfortable. Afraid. He was not acting like the friend she had expected him to be. Then he suddenly smiled and the discussion continued as they talked of mutual friends and the gossip surrounding others they knew. She offered him a drink in the drawing room, but he refused, indicating he had an appointment. Giving her a small peck on the cheek he put on his hat and went out the door.

Rowena was grateful she hadn't had to spend more time with him. The whole day had left her feeling dizzy and unsettled and he'd done nothing to ease her discomfort. She wanted to believe Bradley was the same man she'd always known. A man with a dark humor, but harmless. He had changed. Lately she was no longer sure he only played at being the villain.

She rubbed her arms as a sudden chill wrapped around her. The cold had nothing to do with the weather. Darkness, tainted with something fetid.

———

CHAPTER FOURTEEN

Rowena glanced at the clock as she quickly rose from bed. Margaret, flushed and breathless, was pulling one of her working gowns from the wardrobe. "He said you must come, my lady, though I told him you were asleep at half five in the mornin'. Said he was sent by Mr. Swanson and he'll not leave without you."

"You did right to wake me, Margaret," Rowena slipped into the dress and waited as the young woman helped her fasten the buttons. She wrapped her hair into a careless bun at the nape of the neck, and then pulled on a sturdy pair of boots. I'll create a scandal wearing working boots in public," she joked in an unsuccessful effort to relieve the tension.

Margaret giggled. "I'm afraid it's too late, my lady. I was talking to cook and she told me the Fairchild's is already thinkin' you're quite a *rebel*. At least that's the word they used in front of Grace the day maid."

Rowena hurried down the stairs to the PC who stood waiting in the hallway by the door.

"I've been told to take you straight away to George Yard Buildings in Whitechapel. A woman is dead and I been told you needed to see before they cart her off."

Rowena climbed into her carriage, followed by the young man who couldn't look her in the eyes. She knew he disapproved and riding with her seemed to make him uncomfortable. "Who sent you?"

"Word came through CID. I was told Chief Inspector Swanson himself left the instructions."

"Did you see what had happened to the woman?"

"No, my lady. I was at the offices when we received the call, and then I was dispatched to come direct to you. The

175

desk man told me she was found only a while ago and I had to get you there before they moved her off."

Rowena leaned back, preparing herself for what would come. She was sure the PC wasn't informing her of everything he knew, but she wouldn't ask further questions. They would arrive soon enough. "Thank you for coming so quickly, then."

As the carriage pulled in front of the building, she noted a small crowd of dock workers had already gathered in the street. They had probably been searching for a job in the early hours and stopped to mingle with a growing number of constables. As she stepped from the coach and passed through the men, she could hear a buzz of disapproval. A constable stood outside the entry to the building, but didn't ask her name. In deference to those who permitted her access, she wouldn't have given it anyway. Chalk-faced PC's were descending the stairway as she climbed to the landing where the woman lay. She stepped forward but several moved to form a uniform-clad barrier, blocking her view.

"Who are you?" A ruddy faced man stepped between her and the beat officers.

"Doctor Radcliffe and you are?"

"Reid. Inspector. H Division. I heard you'd be coming but not so quick."

Rowena nodded acknowledgement. "May I take a closer look?"

"It's not natural, you being here," he said before he stepped aside to allow her access to the scene. "Let the doctor see. It is not a pretty sight."

She stepped closer, examining the position of the body. One of the constables reached down to straighten the woman's skirt. "No, please, leave it as it is. I want to take a closer look." Glancing at the floor she looked for blood before stooping down to examine the woman's torso.

There were more than thirty strikes of a sharp instrument. Most had been driven into the chest and abdomen, others into the pelvis. Blood had already begun to stiffen the cloth that surrounded the wounds. Glancing up, Rowena bit her lip when she realized this was one of the prostitutes she'd tended on occasion, though she couldn't remember her name. She had seen her recently with the one they called Pearly Poll or maybe it was Annie Chapman.

The clatter of footsteps announced the arrival of Doctor Killeen. "Get back woman. What do you think you are doing?"

He snorted as he grasped her shoulder and tried to pull her up, back away from the body. "You've no business here, gawking."

DI Reid stepped forward. "Doctor Killen, this is Doctor Radcliffe. She's here at the special request of some powerful people. Best let her have her look, then you can get on with your job."

"Thank you, but I've seen enough. If you'll both excuse me."

Their raucous laughter followed her down the steps to the street, where it seemed a few more people had gathered. Constables who were usually on their way home at this hour jostled for a position that would afford them a better look. In the crowd several women displayed their *goods* trying to interest any of the men in trade. No one seemed to be very concerned about the small crowd, but it sent a chill through her. To well she remembered the crowds that had started small and swelled on Black Sunday. Anxious to leave, she caught her driver's eye and he quickly joined her, pushing aside the spectators, then guiding her safely to the carriage.

———

The killer watched from the back of

the crowd as the prying witch arrived and rushed up the stairs where one of the hags lay. There were others on the list and all had been to see the high-and-mighty lady doctor. Though when all the others were dead, it might be interesting to add a bit of fun, slitting the doctor's throat. She really counted for so little in the scheme of things.

This kill was sloppy and unfinished, but more practice will result in the work of art I intend. I wonder if that slut will know it is her fault and that I am coming for her.

The crowd stirred, some of the gawkers turning away as the PC's began to question everyone. The killer knew it would be too dangerous to stay, and joined a small group as they walked across the street, turning at the first corner in an effort to escape the inquiries of the police.

———

"Thank you for interceding with Doctor Killeen for me. I doubt he would have given me permission to further examine Martha Tabram had you not.

Doctor Anderson looked over at Donald Swanson. "Yes, well, umph...you're most welcome. Killeen is a fine man, an excellent doctor, and I understand he was most outraged you attended the scene. However, I believe he'll be happy to cooperate fully in the future should the need arise." He glanced at the watch he pulled from his pocket. "Um, well must go, appointment you know. Swanson, be a good man and take her statement. Unofficially of course. My lady." He nodded as she rushed out the door.

Swanson hesitated as a look of discomfort flashed across his face. "I don't know if I should say I'm glad to see you or that I'm sorry you had to be called."

Rowena gave a slight nod, acknowledging his concern.

He offered her a chair before he sat across from her. "So tell me, what do you think? Was the killer the one you seek?"

"I'm afraid it is. He's become more proficient at his craft. I suspect he has had more practice since the last victim I examined. Tabram's abdomen was only stabbed, unlike the mutilation in Oxford but I believe he is practicing to see what suits him best. However, the pattern of the attack indicates it is the same murderer and verifies my thoughts that he was coming to London."

"What patterns? There are a number of differences."

"Doctor Killeen's assessment that the killing blow came late in the attack seems apparent. There would not have been so much blood from the wounds had it happened earlier. The man I believe is doing this likes to toy with his victims. I think he knows where he can cause the most damage to weaken his prey while keeping her from fighting him. Escaping. Calling for help."

"How do you know she didn't fight or scream? I certainly can't tell by just looking at the body."

"But you can. You can see she didn't fight, just by looking at her. There were only superficial cuts on her hands and arms. If she was fighting for her life, she would have tried to stop the knife from penetrating her body, raising her hands and arms to ward off the assault, even grasping the blade itself with her hand. There would have been far more damage."

Swanson encouraged her to continue.

"As to crying out, the witnesses said they heard nothing to draw their attention. One even stepped over her on his way to his rooms. If the estimated time of death is correct, he walked over her at close to the same time she died. He insisted he heard nothing and saw no one as he prepared for work or after he walked down the stairs from his room. He would likely have been able to hear a cry. The narrow stairwell would carry the sound upward."

"So, perhaps she was asleep when the attack began and her mouth was covered to keep her from making any noise?"

"No, she would have fought to remove the villain's hand. She would have awakened at his very touch, though she may have passed out from drink. She was a woman who lived on the streets. People develop survival mechanisms such as waking instantly when touched or threatened. The poor who must sleep in alleys and doorways often display this reaction. It's how they survive."

Swanson nodded. "I've seen that reaction when constables rouse the drunks and homeless on the streets. It only takes the lightest touch to get them up and moving along."

I can think of only two reasons she would not have screamed. She was in a drunken stupor so she couldn't feel what happened when her attacker started to stab her. I don't believe this is the case. Had she been so deep into the throes of alcohol and had no *feeling* she would have already been very near death."

"Fascinating. Please go on."

"The other possibility is her killer knew exactly where to strike to disable her ability to speak. This might occur if the first thrust was to the lungs. She would be struggling to breathe and fighting to clear blood from her throat."

"So you think this person knows where these organs are within the body and could accurately strike out and hit these...targets?"

"Yes. I do indeed. The placement of the other blows enforces my belief. Although the rogue is striking, fury building, the depth and placement of the wounds indicate they all hit something vital. Even those to the genital area appeared to have been deliberate. However, as I believe you know, I don't think the same fury was present when those particular blows were struck."

———

CHAPTER FIFTEEN

Rowena sat at the back of the room as the coroner began the inquest. What she heard only confirmed most of what she already knew. Mary Tabram had been found on the staircase landing in a section of the George Yard Buildings, near the small rooms she'd renovated for her surgery. A laborer by the name of John Reeves had discovered her as he left for work, and had immediately run to find a policeman.

There was some confusion about the time of death. Doctor Killeen estimated she had died at approximately 2:30, three hours before he arrived to examine her. However another resident had gone up those same stairs, and seen what must have been Mary asleep. He noticed no blood, and there was no evidence he tracked any to his room.

Rowena leaned close to Garret. "Killeen's time is wrong. The blood was too fresh when I arrived and the changes caused by death, the rigor, had not begun."

"I'm not sure Alfred Crow's statement that he saw no blood is enough to disregard Killeen."

"It's not *just* the blood," she whispered forcefully. "The buildings smell of food and sewage, but you've been near those who've recently died. Unless the witness has no sense of smell, she couldn't have been dead when he passed. The blood and other bodily fluids would have been *very* noticeable. Their scent would have overpowered every other odor and he would have been overcome."

The coroner peered at them from the dais with disgust written on his face, as he turned back to the witness.

Rowena motioned de Grey she wished to leave. He rose and led her out of the room.

"I think you should talk to

Swanson," he said before she had time to add more. "The witnesses outside the building will have to be questioned again. When do you think she died?"

She didn't have the opportunity to answer, as Donald Swanson walked out of the inquest to join them. Garret quickly explained Rowena's opinion. The doctor's testimony was flawed. "I believe she must have died later, closer to three-thirty or four in the morning. There are too many facts pointing to a later time."

"Is there any other reason you doubt his accuracy?" Swanson asked, as he followed the couple outside.

"You saw the position of the body. I have a difficult time believing Crow wouldn't have mentioned it. It would have caused him a fair amount of difficulty to get around her, much less leave him clean of any blood traces."

"If you're correct, I'm afraid the effort to prepare a line-up of sailors will be wasted, though I admit I believe it is a futile effort to have the witness attempt identification. As you know we cannot be positive about the time of the event, and the Connelly woman is certainly not very reliable."

"I don't envy you and your

investigators. All the hard work you must do to follow-up on what are usually inaccurate or incorrect reports."

"Yes, well it's just part of the job."

"Would you care to join us for coffee, Swanson?" de Grey offered.

Rowena shot him a glance. No such plan had been agreed between them, but she extended the offer as well.

The Chief Inspector declined, assuring them he'd direct his detectives to conduct additional interviews. Leaving them standing on the building steps, he hurried to his carriage.

———

The general public didn't appear to take much notice of the gruesome killing and the stories quickly disappeared from the news pages. The daily routines at the surgery, which had been disrupted for a few days following the murder, returned to normal. The few people who knew Mary Tabram mourned only briefly, even Rowena's patients who had called her their friend. Tabram had been a difficult woman when she was drinking and she had frequently indulged.

Rowena submersed herself in work, refusing invitations, keeping long hours at the surgery. Portia worked with her to assure there was always someone available should she be called away. At night she had nightmares, though she would never admit it. She would awaken from dreams of the faceless killer, knife held high, ready to strike. On the rare occasion she encountered de Grey, she would escape as quickly as she could, as he searched her eyes with his own. She refused to admit how heavy her heart had become as she waited for the fiend to strike again.

———

"I'm telling you, she's not well. This killing. It's scorched her soul. I warned you. You have to retract your permission." De Grey tried to keep the desperation from his voice.

Albany huffed. "She recovered from the others, she'll recover from this. She is not weak and I'll not interfere. She was correct in her assumptions, though I do not understand how she could have known, been so sure. She's *earned* the right to continue as she asked." Albany's eyes were steel and it was clear he would not stand for an argument.

"Then you must put a stop to this recklessness. I've watched her work late into the night in those vial and dangerous rooms.   She walks down the streets, searching for the men and women who refuse her services by any other method."

"I'll speak with her, but I warn you, you'll be the first she'll suspect of making these demands. It will not make it easier for you to grow closer."

"Excuse me, your grace," Swanson said from the chair he occupied, forgotten as the struggle of wills between the two men had raged. "I'm sorry de Grey, but I think you're wrong. Lady Radcliffe is only reacting to what has occurred as any normal woman or *man* would do. Nor is she in any additional danger. You have your men watching her closely. She has done nothing she has not done before."

Albany smiled. "Go on."

"I admit I was against including her in our investigation.   Though I held my tongue I was outraged you would make such a request, but she has been right about everything she's told us. Even about the time the Tabram woman was killed."

De Grey stared at the man, fighting to keep his temper under control. "You know this how?"

"I had a long talk with Killeen and when pressed he admitted he had...misstated the time of death.   If it hadn't been for the Lady Radcliffe, we would have wasted even more time chasing shadows."

"So you want her more involved? In more danger?" Garret wanted to wring the man's neck, but knew it was an overreaction to what he was hearing.

Swanson bit back an oath, inhaling deeply before turning to respond to de Grey. "Of course he doesn't. He just wants you to calm down and leave this alone for now."

Albany walked across the room and poured a drink breaking the tension that electrified the air. Ignoring the look on Garret's face, he settled into the chair at his desk.

Garret looked over at his grace and sat down, struggling to maintain a professional demeanor, trying to accept his defeat with dignity. "I'll do as you ask your grace. Swanson, you make a formidable opponent." He smiled. "I have to wonder why you've always appeared so meek."

Swanson grinned. "I learned my lesson in the gambling halls when I was young. Never show anyone all your cards."

Garret burst into laughter. "You must be very hard to beat at cards."

———

"Get out! Get out of my sight before I flay you and strip your flesh to your bones!" Sheffield screamed at the man he'd sent to Rowena's home with a special invitation.

The man scampered from the hall.

"My lord, you mustn't allow that ungrateful woman to upset you so."

"Shut up, Morgana. I don't want to hear from you either. You forget your place of late."

"I beg your forgiveness. I spoke out of turn."

He waved her out of the room, and stared at the picture above the fireplace. His father, long dead, stared back at him. He'd hated the man and been grateful for his early death. It had saved him the trouble of finding a way to eliminate the old bastard.

The fool, running around spending my inheritance on charitable causes.

He had to laugh, as he found himself making offers to Rowena to support those she was so fond of. Of course offering a servant to assist her in her endeavors cost little. The hag needed something to do now that the travel with his nieces and nephews was over.

Rage swept through him and he threw the glass at his father's picture. *Rowena. Just who do you think you are, refusing my invitations?*

He stared off into the distance. Actors in the play entered the stage of his imagination. He closed his eyes to watch as the woman learned how hopeless her little causes were, and discovered there was no hope she would survive his ire. His lips twisted in an evil smile. *Yes, Rowena, now is the time. Always expect the worst.*

CHAPTER SIXTEEN

It had been less than a month, and once again she was called to the scene of mutilation and heart-wrenching tragedy. It was harder to look at this woman whose throat had been slashed and abdomen splayed open. Much harder, she knew Mary Ann Nichols well. She had been among her first and most loyal patients. Occasionally called Polly by her friends, her trust had opened the doors for Rowena as she searched for a way to help the poor unfortunate women.

Inspector Spratling glared at her as she walked toward the body. "Stand back. You may have blessing to be here, but you'll wait until I finish my review."

Dr. Llewellyn, who'd hurried from his carriage just as she'd arrived, stood next to her. "I don't believe his comments are what you may think. He allowed me only to pronounce her life extinct, and then told me to step aside as well."

Rowena knew the smile she gave him bore more sadness than the thanks it was meant to convey. "I haven't had the opportunity to get to know you well before. I'm sad it has to be under such circumstances."

"It must be difficult, being a woman and trying to make a difference. I understand you've conducted many studies on the minds and methods of the deranged who commit these abomi...no, who kill. I don't think there has ever been another so violent."

Rowena watched the man blanch as he looked over at the corpse again. "I understand your cousin is trying to pursue a medical career. Is she bent on flaunting established practices as I have, or shall she take up nursing and become a merciful angel?"

It was his turn to show a weak smile. "She's following in my footsteps. I'm surprised you know of her. We do not travel in your circles, my lady."

"I'm always aware of young and capable women who are dedicated to the healing practices."

"Alright, you can take your gander," Inspector Spratling called out as he stepped around the body to speak with the constables standing along the street. The men were trying to ignore the victim and the smell of death that floated on the gathering fog.

"You notice the killer struck at the neck twice." Llewellyn pointed out two distinct cuts along the side of Nichols neck.

"Perhaps he hesitated as he began the attack, yet any discomfort he may have had at striking in such a way was quickly overcome. I overheard Constable Neil telling his fellow he heard nothing as he walked toward this spot. If the blood was indeed still flowing from the wounds as he insisted, he had to have been on the very heels of the assailant." Rowena glanced down at the gaping abdomen.

"Do you think it's the same man who killed that poor immoral creature when last we met? The wounds are not the same."

Rowena bit her lip, holding back a retort. *Immoral? What gives him the right to make such a judgment?* "Mary Tabram was stabbed numerous times, and there's no immediate evidence that occurred here, but we'll know better after a full examination is made. But I'd say it's the same killer, that he's playing games as he practices his...craft."

Llewellyn stood back until she finished.

Rowena crouched down to have a better look...taking time to closely examine the wounds. There was evidence the murderer had sliced through the skin efficiently, but the muscle layer was cut in jagged start and stop motions. Standing she stepped aside for Llewellyn.

After he completed a cursory examination, he stepped to her side. "I must call for the mortuary wagon. You're welcome to join me in a closer exam, should that be your desire."

"I will."

"I don't mean to dishonor you with this question, but how can you, a lady of privilege, look at this horror?"

"I see the damage that was done, and it's most gruesome. But, I also see the soul of the person who's died as it hovers close and begs us to find justice for her as well. It is imagining the person she could have been in life that brings me here, and gives me hope the knowledge I gain will make it easier to find those who callously destroy the lives of others."

___

Storm. The endearment for Garret de Grey slipped too easily to her lips of late and the desire she had once felt again made its presence known. Her heart beat faster as she watched him stride purposefully up the staircase to the first floor where she stood at the drawing room door, issuing instructions for the dinner. His broad chest and narrow waist were accented by the black brocade Regency tailcoat. She couldn't help remembering all other times she had seen him looking so handsome.

"Have you lost your mind? You're going to bring Sheffield into the heart of the investigation. Did he mesmerize you into providing this sick entertainment?"

She'd learned, at a more tender age, when he was in this mood it was best to let the temperamental tirade wear out before trying to respond to questions that challenged her activities. "De Grey. I see you decided to join us this evening."

Garret ignored her words. "You've always been an odd one, Rowena. You didn't take well to your introduction to society. You never wished to simper behind your fan and find the right man to tame you. I'm surprised the earl left you the fortune he did. He wasn't happy with your choices."

Rowena shrugged as she walked to the drawing room, Garret following. "True, but he was happy with his only child."

At the doorway she gestured he precede her.

"Bloody hell, he must often turn over in his grave as he watches you walk the dangerous streets and give care to the unfortunates. You had to go to that heathen country, America, for your training to doctor. And why you decided on a career is well beyond my comprehension. Now you've insinuated yourself into this foul mess."

She smiled her best debutant smile and was happy she avoided gritting her teeth as she entered the room. Walking to the sideboard she silently gestured to the whiskey and raised an eyebrow in question.

"I'll pour my own," he snapped, walking to her side and dropping the cane he held in his hand into the ornamental brass stand set beside the cabinet for that purpose.

His eyes gleamed with cooling anger as he took a strangle hold on the decanter neck and poured a generous portion.

"I'm not entertaining anyone here tonight, Storm. It's a gathering of minds bent to the same purpose, finding a killer and stopping him."

"But Sheffield-

She held her finger to his lips, hushing him. "Sheffield often provides insights we may not otherwise suggest. He leans toward a darker side. I'm very aware of this. Yet as far as I know, he has never harmed anyone or anything in answer to this more chilling side of his nature. This makes him a valuable asset to such a discussion. He doesn't try to hide his somewhat immoral thoughts." *And I hope*

I'm not making a mistake trusting him. I need Thomas's opinion to confirm my suspicions or ease my mind. Storm would not be so angry if he knew my true purpose in inviting Bradley.

Storm's hand clasped hers as he pulled her finger from his lips. "I hate to admit it, but you may be right. Perhaps he can be helpful, though I doubt it seriously."

Voices on the staircase drifted into the room. "I believe some of the others have arrived. Are you in control of your temper, or shall I forestall their arrival so you can gather your thoughts?" she teased, watching the tension bleed from his shoulders.

Rather than answer, he sipped at his whiskey and walked across the room to look out the window as Lord Bradley Sheffield and Donald Swanson entered the room, followed by Doctor Llewellyn. As the gentlemen took up glasses, a fifth man arrived and stood in the doorway. His stout build and balding head might have caused people to overlook him unless they noticed the intensity in his eyes.

"Thomas, I am so glad you were able to come," Rowena said taking his arm and leading him to a comfortable chair. "Gentlemen, this is Doctor Thomas Bond of

199

Westminster. He and I have been corresponding during the past year. He's a police surgeon and shares some of my thoughts on the criminal mind. He also advocates the theory you can determine who a killer is a thorough an assessment of the victims."

Swanson offered his hand to the man, "I've heard of your theories. I believe you also work with another man...Phillips. George Phillips if I remember correctly."

"And are you one our detractors, or have you opened your mind to such possibilities?" Doctor Bond asked.

"I hope to have an open mind, but what you're suggesting is somewhat unusual. Are you saying the murdered victims are at fault in drawing these people to them?"

"Not at all, it is more-"

"Gentlemen, there will be plenty of time for this discussion after dinner. Margaret is at the door to let us know all is ready. I believe, though you are all strong of stomach, we should discuss this over a drink after dessert."

Sheffield stepped forward and took Rowena's arm, his glance at Garret one of triumph.

They led the small procession to the

dining room. Silver and crystal sparkled on the table, which held savory pyramids of fruit and bowls of fragrant flowers aligned along the center of its broad lace-covered surface. The fare which sat on the sideboard was hardy--hare soup, turkey, lamb and a variety of side accompaniments filled the room with their individual aromas and mixed to form mouthwatering scents. Each course was served quickly and efficiently as they sipped their wine and became acquainted during the meal. They abided Rowena's wish to delay the more interesting matters until the repast was complete.

When dinner ended she led everyone to the library, with its masculine furnishings and book-lined shelves, knowing they would be more comfortable here than in the other rooms. Giving them permission to smoke as she helped herself to a sherry, she glanced at the five men. "As I explained to Lord de Grey before you arrived, I believe each of us has some insight about this monster. I have asked you to be present in the hope that together we can find justice for those he's killed."

"Well, I for one do not see what all the hue and cry is about," Bradley Sheffield declared, glancing at Rowena. "It's only two whores on the streets who died in a nasty way."

Donald Swanson reddened, as he, too, glanced at the woman sitting in their midst, then accepted the challenge to explain. "There are several factors that make it necessary to determine who is responsible for these crimes. First and above all else is the very fact these women were murdered. Not by the hand of a drunken customer or husband, which is not so unusual among these people, but by some person they may never have met nor seen before. Moreover, the murders have occurred in a sensational and morbid manner. Citizens who live in the more comfortable homes abutting the district are nervous and afraid. They cry out to have protection and a quick resolution."

"But they have been unaffected. Normally they would be outraged having a word of such occurrences reach their tender ears," Sheffield laughed grimly before taking a sip of his drink.

"Yes," Lord de Grey, acknowledged, "but times are different since the riots of Black Sunday. The news mongers have been searching for something to sensationalize. I would say they're doing an excellent job with these killings. The papers have carried the stories in a manner similar to the way they publish a bawdy novel. They tell every outrageous detail of what has occurred and been said by every person involved."

Margaret entered the room with a cart laden with coffee, tea, cakes, and other delicacies.

"Thank you," Rowena said."Just put them in front of the desk. Our guests can help themselves as they wish," Rowena directed. Turning back to the men, "I believe it may be a long evening of discovery, disagreement, and theorizing and I would not wish you gentlemen to want for anything."

"In other words, you want your staff to be able to retire instead of awaiting our call," Sheffield retorted. "You're much too gracious to your servants." He laughed as she glanced at him through cat slit eyes.

"Yes. Well, what do you think this little group can accomplish the Yard and London Police cannot, dear girl?" Dr. Bond asked, aware of his role at this gathering and ready to move things along.

Rowena set her sherry aside as she explained. "I'm not sure we can accomplish any outcome, but perhaps we can provide insights we haven't had before.

Chief Inspector Swanson may not have the time to formulate all the various approaches the investigation may require. I believe pressures are building on the Metropolitan, with the public and with the killer. Doctor Bond, perhaps you would like to share some of your theories?"

"My beliefs have not been well received by the investigators," he said walking across the room. Stopping by the tea cart, he poured a cup of coffee and selected several of the finger sandwiches and pastries set out, before returning to his chair. He glanced up to see all eyes on him. "Mr. Swanson, I actually sent some general information to one of your superiors after the first killing, based on some studies I've conducted. It was not well received."

"I've not heard anything of this," the Chief Inspector said as he sipped at the last of the whiskey he'd poured when they'd entered the room. "Please, go ahead. I'd like to hear what you have to say."

As she noticed Bond's reluctance to begin, Rowena explained, "Thomas and I have formulated similar ideas. I believe you can determine the mental engagement of a killer through the actions he takes to commit his crime."

Storm looked cynical, but didn't interrupt as she continued.

"Thomas believes you can garner information about the physical traits of the killer by the manner in which the killing is accomplished."

Lord Sheffield buffed his nails against the lapel of his maroon smoking jacket then glanced down at his hands, "Go on, this is astounding," he muttered a look of disdain on his face.

"Yes, please," Swanson encouraged. "What are your ideas on the matter of these traits and how do you arrive at these conclusions?"

Thomas Bond sat back in his chair, balancing the steaming coffee on his knee and straightening his tie as he placed his finger into the high, wing top collar of his shirt, and pulled at it gently.

owena had noticed this was a common mannerism he had and was sure he wasn't even aware how often he practiced the mannerism. "I'm sure you'd agree there are some physical traits necessary to accomplish what you've seen in these killings. A significant amount of strength is required. It's not easy to slice someone's neck through to the spine. It's my understanding you saw this in one of your victims. A person would have to be of a size and age that would permit them to do this as well. For example, a cripple whose legs are useless couldn't reach the height needed for these actions."

Donald nodded, encouraging Bond to continue tapping his pipe against his hand, then using a tamper to pack the tobacco before lighting it.

"Of course I haven't seen the victims, so I can speak only to what Doctor Radcliffe has told me and what I've seen at similar scenes. I'd suspect the killer has to be male, who has sufficient height to stand equal to or above these women. I believe only a man is physically strong enough for these murders."

"That makes a certain amount of sense." de Grey glanced toward Rowena, eyebrow raised and a conspiratorial smile on his lips. "But could it be a woman? There are many who are of sufficient height and some could be...strong."

Lord Sheffield, who had risen to take tea and help himself to a few of the delicacies, coughed. Quickly setting down the biscuit he'd just bitten into, he sipped the steaming tea, then finally spoke. "Excuse me. I believe a bit of this sweet lodged uncomfortably. You were saying?"

Thomas glanced back at de Grey, "No, certainly not, it must be a man. A woman wouldn't have the stomach for such gruesome attacks. Nor would she have the strength required."

"I can't agree with those statements," Rowena said thoughtfully. "A woman would certainly have the ability to kill with the fury we saw in the Mary Tabram killing and such anger could give them added strength. And I've seen my laundress lift bundles of cleaning that I'm sure are quite heavy, which would indicate she could have the strength to do such a thing. Why, with one of my surgical instruments sharply honed, I could inflict such damage." She laughed.

The men looked at her in disbelief. "Have you determined what the weapon is, Inspector?" Bradley said settling back into his seat with his tea, but he'd left the delicacies he selected sitting on a small plate he'd set on the desk.

The men erupted into a vigorous discussion regarding the various types of instruments which could have been used to commit the murders. When Thomas Bond disagreed with Doctor Killeen's suggestion more than one knife had been used, the talk became even livelier. Having familiarity only with her own surgical tools rather than the wide variety of other deadly weapons they were discussing, she half listened.

Something else was bothering her and, though she hadn't broached the subject this evening, it worried her greatly. The first and second killings had been less than a month apart. The police had no real evidence or witness accounts to help them find the killer and citizens were beginning to offer a variety of rewards. Add to this the wild speculation being published in the news and fantastic tales woven by the reporters, the waters were being muddied.

She was satisfied DI Abberline and his partners would do their best to stay on course. In the storm of speculation, however they could only work with the information they possessed. The witnesses were already showing the influence of the wild tales carried on the lips of their neighbors.

There was only one thing she could be certain of. The killer, whoever it turned out to be, would kill again. The only question was how soon.

———

CHAPTER SEVENTEEN

Lord Bradley Sheffield dropped his jacket across the arms of his butler Galt, dismissing the old, nearly deaf man with a flick of his wrist. He chuckled to himself, thinking of soft-hearted Rowena and her caring, tender ways with her servants. The hour was late, or early depending on how one judged such things, but the one thing he was sure of, his servants were available to serve his needs at any hour of the day.

Satisfied he had worn Rowena down, as evidenced by this evening's invitation, he was energized by the discussions that had taken place. He bypassed his rooms and continued up the back staircase to where Morgana's rooms were found. As expected, he found her kneeling in prayer at the side of her bed.

"You're a wicked sinner," he greeted her harshly. "I've come to punish you for your sins."

Morgana stood, bowing her head, a muttered thank you on her lips. "My lord, you shall help me to save my soul and ascend to the hands of God."

"I do not want your thanks," he growled, taking her arm and forcing her back to her knees. "You caused Lady Radcliffe much difficulty. You didn't do as she directed and she forced you from your duty. I spoke with her briefly tonight about your disobedience. You nearly cost me entry to the circle I need to play the game. You must make amends."

Morgana glanced up, her eyes glowing with triumph. "I am ashamed, my lord."

Sheffield glared at her a moment, then his eyes softened with pleasure. "I do so enjoy the play, my Morgana, and tonight will be a performance even you will be satisfied with." Reaching down he yanked her hair, forcing her back to her feet. Tearing away the thin material of her gown, he pushed her flat upon the narrow bed. Taking his time to assure she was safely secured, he took the small whip from the foot of the bed and began to enjoy one of his favorite entertainments.

Rowena stood inside the mortuary as the coffin was placed in the hearse. Several of Mary Nichol's friends and family members huddled beside a cart arranged to carry them to the burial site. Of those gathered, she only recognized Catherine and Mary Jane who appeared quieter than the rest of those standing around. She saw them nervously glancing at the others who were present and supposed they were intimidated by their lofty offices.

There were representatives of the press, Detective Inspector Abberline, and several other investigators she didn't recognize. Chief Inspector Swanson, Doctors Llewellyn and Killeen were also present, as was Storm de Grey. Most surprising was the presence of Lord Bradley Sheffield and his servant, Morgana Ridley. Rowena made a point of ignoring the woman and noted the cynical smile on Sheffield's face when she realized he was watching her.

De Grey helped her into the

carriage that followed the hearse. The heady scent of the flowers Rowena had ordered to drape the box barely covered the odor of decay that pervaded the courtyard. Family and friends of the dead woman, who had apparently fortified themselves with drink before attending, stumbled and laughed as they finally climbed into their pitifully shabby cart.

"What is *he* doing here and why would he bring the woman?" de Grey asked acidly, speaking in a low voice meant only for her ears.

"I image Morgana wished to pay her respects. She knows several of the women from the surgery. Perhaps she wishes to add her prayers. She has a...deep faith. As for Sheffield, I suppose he used his contacts to assure he'd be comfortable having gained entry to this group. He wouldn't care to fight through the crowd of spectators."

Rowena watched the pair as Sheffield stepped into the last carriage, followed by Morgana who surprisingly took a seat next to the man. The police representatives and medical men also crowded into the remaining seats, leaving the reporters to walk behind or along the sides of the carriages.

"I'm not as generous as you. I believe both of them are here only for their own sordid pleasure. You said the woman displayed disgust for you patients, so why would she be sad one has expired?"

"Storm, stop. This isn't the time or place to show your temper." Rowena sat back as the carriage rolled forward. Looking over her shoulder, she noted there was a larger crowd than she had anticipated for the woman's final journey. People pressed forward at the sight of the small procession. Constables, at the gate and along the road, worked to clear a path for the conveyances.

"Look at these people. Who are they? You can be assured they didn't know the Nichols woman," Storm criticized.

"It astounds me as well. Unfortunately I don't believe they're here to mourn, though that may be what they tell themselves."

"So, why are they here blocking the roads?"

"Entertainment, like Sheffield, fear of death or the killer, a few are truly sorry and wish to offer their prayers and support to those she left behind."

"You've grown quite knowledgeable about the workings of people's minds,

Row."

A smile curved her lips. "Not really, the more I've learned what drives some people the easier it is to accept certain odd behaviors. Most people fear death and acting as a spectator to an event such as this assures them they're alive. A showing like this makes it more difficult for the detectives. They must feel they're on a carousel as they work through all the reports and sightings of this monster and see all these people clamoring for answers. How can they manage?"

"I understand from Swanson there are hundreds of reports of suspicious actors. Several seem to be under serious consideration," Storm offered.

The cries from the crowds along the street made it difficult to talk for several minutes.

He glanced back to the carriage where Swanson sat. "I'm surprised Dr. Anderson isn't in attendance. He usually thrives on being in the public eye. Though there is little glory in this, perhaps he wished to distance himself."

Rowena glanced over at one of the reporters who ran along beside the carriage holding the mourners. "Donald told me his superior is suffering from some illness and was to leave today for Switzerland to have treatments. I believe Chief Swanson is being abandoned, held out as a sacrificial lamb. He'll be blamed should the killing continue without resolution."

"You may be right about Donald. I don't envy the position he's placed in."

"Now I have a question for you. Why are *you* here, my lord?"

"Me? I have been assisting with the investigations."

Rowena studied Storm's eyes, expecting humor but finding none. "You've played a part in this since I first became interested in these killings. Are you truly *that* interested in this monster or do you have some other mission?"

"You continue to ask questions that are difficult to answer. I'm interested." He glanced away from her searching eyes. "I'm interested in the mind of a demon that can do such deadly damage. It's your fault, really."

"My fault?"

The carriage slowed as it entered the dismal grounds of the cemetery where the coffin and its sad contents would be laid to rest. The roadway was heavily rutted and it was difficult to talk until the

215

carriage bounced to a halt.

"Yes. I became interested when we were young and you could so easily read the real nature of those around you. I always kept abreast of the activities of those you accused of having a darker soul. I'm sad to admit I haven't found you to be wrong even once."

"I remember you when you are hardly taller than a pony, Row. You wanted to always help everyone then you discovered how evil some people can be. It was a terrible time for you and I couldn't help you then, I don't know if I can do anything to help you now. But you have to take care there are things outside this carriage that will crush you."

She wanted to ask more but it would have to wait as the horses came to a stop. Joining the few friends of the victim at the graveside, she lowered her head as the minister droned his prayers. The service was blessedly short. Soon the gravediggers appeared ready to fill the dark hole in the ground. Shortly, as the mourners and onlookers watched solemnly, the casket was lowered into the ground.

———

CHAPTER EIGHTEEN

Wednesdays she usually took away from the surgery for personal errands. She'd already been to the dressmaker for a fitting, and stopped at several of the other shops on her list, when she noticed the new coffee house had opened. Entering it she selected a seat away from the window but close enough to enjoy the parade of shoppers as they passed by.

DI Abberline entered and she saw him immediately. He could be pursuing some miscreant, or just taking an afternoon period to relax Unsure, she didn't call out to him. To her delight he walked over, asking to share her table.

"We've had little opportunity to talk together, away from murder scenes and the rush of an active CID office. Do you mind if we talk about your theories?" At her invitation he selected the chair that permitted him to sit with his back against the wall.

She'd noticed it was a common practice with police, sitting where they had a view of all the activity in the room. "Actually I'm glad to have the opportunity to talk with you away from your office. I'm wondering what your opinions are regarding the killer."

"I try not to form opinions. They have a way of sending an investigation in the wrong direction."

"Oh, perhaps I misstated. Why do you think these women have been the target of this madman?"

"It's difficult to tell. The most common reasons a woman on the street is killed, is someone wants the money they've earned, or their husband or lover becomes drunk and takes their usual battering too far. Occasionally you'll see some lunatic who attacks for no obvious reason."

"Do you think this may be the case here?"

"In honesty, I have to say I think it's too early in the investigation to know. We've almost no information on who is making these attacks. My private feeling is we don't have a lunatic. These killings have been planned. The cutthroat shows organization and has prepared a manner of escape."

A waiter approached and took Abberline's order.

"Then you agree with some of my theories, you can determine the nature of a killer by the way he kills and the victims he chooses."

Rowena sat quietly waiting as Abberline's drink arrived and he took a sip from the cup.

"I believe your theories are as worthless as the fingerprints that Fauld's fellow suggested we use a few years back. Those who tout the use of such tools are usually wasting my time. I don't agree with the summaries you provided from your research, but I *do* find you highly intelligent and observant," he smiled ruefully, "which, will I hope keep you from finding me a bore and a charlatan."

Rowena laughed. "Well done. You avoided my ire before I even noticed I should be upset. Does it disturb you then?

That I have access to your investigations?"

"As I just said, I find you intelligent and observant. Your theories may be incorrect, but much of what you said has been along my line of thought. I hear you also were instrumental in finding fault with some of the medical reports and have helped us re-direct our queries. However, I'm not so well impressed by some of your friends."

"You mean Storm...Lord de Grey. I thought his activities are blessed by Dr. Anderson and Chief Swanson."

The room bustled with activity, waiters delivering the tea at tables scattered about the room. Rowena nodded to acquaintances as they passed the table being seated or leaving the café.

"I wasn't speaking of de Grey. He's an important member of the investigative team."

Rowena blinked, wondering what he meant. "De Grey is an important member of the investigation? I thought he was just there to observe." *And irritate me*, she thought.

"I know Swanson spends a fair amount of time with him, but perhaps I am misreading what I see. But as I said it isn't de Grey wanting information, it's your other friend, Lord Sheffield."

"Sheffield? What exactly do you mean?" She hadn't seen Bradley since the funeral and had been relieved he'd not been around nor made demands for her attention.

"He requested copies of a number of reports for you. It takes time to prepare those and we've little enough staff to prepare what is needed for the investigators and our superiors."

Rowena was stunned at the news. Never would she send Bradley on such an errand. She'd worked hard to build the trust of these men only to find he was trying to undermine her relationships. "Detective, I don't know what to say. I...it was a misunderstanding, surely. I would never."

"So I see. Perhaps your friend is really no friend at all. I'll inform the clerk when I return to the station, there's no rush to make the copies. The rest we'll keep between us, unless there is a need to say something."

"You're most gracious. I promise I'll talk to Lord Sheffield myself and make him clearly understand he shouldn't bother you again. So is this why you chose to join me for coffee?"

Abberline smiled. "Of course not. I

really am interested in your thoughts."

"Yet you don't believe my theories have merit."

"I can't really say. The ideas are new to me. I admit I don't accept change well so I'll try to hold off final judgment. Why do *you* think this killer has attacked these women?"

"I agree money, jealousy, love or hate and revenge are the usual reasons to drive a man to kill. However, there are other things as well. The drive to protect what is or is perceived to be his, home, family, business. There are those who kill in the name of religion. However if religion were the case I believe you'd see something to point you in that direction."

"Such as?"

"Letters with quotes from the bible. A cross or medallion which has some religious significance. Then there are those who carve what they considered the mark of their beliefs into the victim or on something nearby."

"You are a student of evil in the heart of men."

"And a woman's. It's not common, but women can also do horrible things to those around them."

The sound of yelling and a clatter of

horse hooves dancing on the street made Rowena glance out the window. A chill crept down her spine when she noticed Morgana Ridley, clutching a bible to her chest, staring in at her with hate-filled eyes.

"You're not suggesting a woman did this. I understand you discussed this with Chief Swanson and discarded the idea." Abberline leaned back in his chair, his face the picture of incredulity.

It took great effort to force her eyes back at the detective. "No, I don't believe a woman has done this. I do however think the police don't always consider all the possibilities." She smiled, casting a glance back at the window. The woman was gone.

"I can't think of a reasonable motivation strong enough to account for these murders. I've certainly met women who are zealous in their religious beliefs. Have a great fear and hatred of the life these unfortunate women lead, but those things don't appear to be reason enough to move them to kill." The images of Morgana who hated and feared the unfortunates flitted through her mind.

Abberline stood. "You've certainly given me many things to ponder, and unfortunately I have an appointment."

"So it seems. I do as well, Detective Inspector." She frowned as her thoughts turned to Lord Sheffield.

He needs to hear exactly what's on my mind.

———

"How *dare* you use my name to gain information about this investigation, Bradley. I can't believe you have the audacity to-"

"Rowena. *Darling.* Really you'll spoil your complexion if you carry on so. It was a harmless enough request. I-"

"Harmless. You've lied to Abberline. You used me, my name as an excuse. Why would you even think I would allow this? Why would you even want access to those reports?"

"Curiosity?"

She didn't believe him and it must have shown on her face.

"Okay, darling. I am feeling so left out and abandoned. You and de Grey know everything and I don't. I know there must be so much more in those reports than you and the papers have released. Really, it's such a little thing to get upset over."

"Bradley, I know you don't believe

what you're saying. If I'd ever said I was doing *anything* at your request, and it was a lie-"

"Alright. I guess you made your point. Gracious such a fuss." He chuckled weakly.

"This is not a laughing matter."

"Rowena, nothing is worth the effort you're making to slap me on the hand. I'm well chastised. Now tell me, what *is* going on in this dreadful investigation you're so protective of? You haven't told me another thing since that awful dinner party at your home."

It had been a very long time since someone made her angry enough to want to scream. "Bradley. I want you to understand me. You. Will. Not. Ever. Do such a thing again."

"I won't," he pouted. "But there's so little to entertain one here in the city. Most everyone has left to their country estates or is traveling abroad."

"You could as well. You've properties across half of England and there's nothing to keep you here."

"Well, I hate to admit it but I did promise Morgana a respite. The journey last year with those children was just devastating if you need to know the truth."

225

"I can't believe I'm hearing this from your lips. You actually care about someone else? She is your employee and I have never once seen you care a whit about what anyone below your station is concerned with. You are no longer traveling with your nieces and nephews."

"I don't care exactly, but I'd hate to lose her talented services, should I go abroad again. It's awful we can't indenture our servants. I had to make a choice. Lose her to some other lord or lady or stay and allow her to recover her wits. I may begin travel again in the fall, but in the meantime, I find her interesting at times and of course her presence does stir up the gossips."

Rowena felt sick at her stomach as she saw the sparkle in Sheffield's eyes. Could he really keep a woman in his home just to cause a stir in society?

"Well it's good of you to care so much for her capabilities." Rowena hoped her words didn't sound as false to Sheffield as they did to her own ears.

Bradley frowned. "So here I am, wasting away as I wait for some madman to strike down another harlot."

———

CHAPTER NINETEEN

   Jame Darbey hated living in London. Hated living in the house with all the people coming and going all hours of the day and night. He wanted to go back to the farm but his new Da' said there was more work in the city. He heard a woman giggling in the courtyard. Kneeling on his cot, he carefully lifted a corner of the waxed butcher paper Mum had put over the window. If Da' saw him, he knew he'd get a great wallapin' but how else was he gonna' learn? He was eleven and almost a man. Peeking out he could see the doxie was drunk as she stumbled about in the light from the street lantern.

The man with her pointed and a moment later she lifted the back of her skirt and placed her hands on the brick wall across from the window. Jame could feel his pants tighten as he got a look at the woman's bare bottom before the man stepped behind her.

Liquid splashed on the wall in front of the woman. He would have laughed at the taller man, who began to lose his stomach in his hat, if the woman hadn't dropped to the ground, her head lolling at an odd angle. Jame wanted to scream when the smaller man looked up at him, a blade glinting in the light from the street, dripping with the same dark fluid. He could barely see the horrifying grin across the man's face as he bent, cut open the clothing and began to hack off part of the woman's body.

Hands over his mouth, Jame dropped down onto his cot next to the window, curled into a ball, eyes staring. Later his mum would wonder what he had seen on that night. He never spoke again.

——

Her heart ached as she looked upon Annie Chapman in the dark, trash-filled yard. A significant crowd had gathered and was yelling insults to the patrol officers. She tried to block the noise from her thoughts as she reviewed the events affecting the murder scene.

John Davis, a lodger in the small dilapidated building had stepped out of the house to find Annie lying beside the steps. Seeing the dead woman, he'd rushed to find the police, instead bringing a lad back to confirm what he'd seen. They called others who were passing to take a look. By the time Mrs. Richardson an elderly neighbor, had gone to the Commercial Police Station, a significant crowd had gathered and almost an hour had passed before Inspector Chandler had arrived.

Though all had sworn they had not touched nor drawn close to the bloody pile, Rowena was certain the scene had been disturbed.

Perhaps the killer had decided stairwells and street corners were becoming too available to discovery and had sought a more private environment for this murder, though he had failed miserably. To make it more difficult the madman had barely given those who cared time to morn Mary Ann Nichols, whose funeral had just occurred the day before.

Doctor George Phillips was attending the scene as she'd arrived. An elderly gentleman who was known for his skills, he didn't approve of her interests, but was gracious enough to step back when she requested he do so. Taking several shallow breaths, attempting to adjust to the scents of death, garbage, and decay she prepared herself to examine a woman she had truly liked.

Moving closer, she locked up her emotions and turned into the professional observer she needed to be to make the exam. She studied the body carefully. The victim's head rested only a few inches from the building's steps. One arm looked posed and rested on a breast. The legs were drawn up and askew. The killer had taken more time with this one. Her throat was cut in a jagged, uneven manner. The open abdomen was similar to what she had observed on the last victim. A portion of the intestines, skin and a large quantity of blood rested just above the woman's left shoulder, and reminded Rowena of the mutilation to the victim outside Oxford. Here, as he'd done that night so many months before, he appeared to have removed the uterus.

One of the constables, pale but

stalwart, held a lantern to give her light as she finished. He then directed her attention to the blood splatters on the wall a distance above the ground. More blood glistened on a woodpile near the body.

Had she tucked up her skirts and bent forward, bracing herself against the wall, waiting to perform? Had she turned, sending the blood onto the wood in the moments she would have lived after the knife had slashed her? She hoped the photographer would be asked to capture these details for further study.

Why did you go so willingly into a dark yard with a killer, Annie?

Of course, she knew the answer. Dark alleys, stairway landings, doorways and poorly lit streets were the business addresses of those who were desperate to live even in these hellish streets.

Annie had been livelier than most of the women she knew who worked in these conditions. She always had a new plot or plans to lift herself up, escape the streets. She would laugh loudly when Rowena admonished her to take care. She and her friends seemed happy enough when they found themselves together at the surgery, joking and teasing each other about their choice of customers, a hat discovered in a

231

trash bin, the offer from a *gentleman* to buy them a pint.

"Lady Radcliffe, you need to make way for the doctor," Inspector Chandler said.

Rowena smiled sadly, all her efforts to learn medicine, the care she had taken with investigators and constables to make them aware of her credentials, but here she was, asked to step aside for *the* doctor once again.

Silly. I accepted Anderson's terms. I am effectively not here, but I didn't think it would hurt like this.

Startled by her own self-pity, she watched as the ambulance attendants carefully lifted Annie into the wagon and took her away.

———

Rowena stepped down from her carriage onto the sidewalk. Looking up she was surprised to find Storm watching her from the top step as she began the climb to his level.

"You look as though you could use some rest."

"Do I look bad? You never were one to hold back your opinion, were you Storm?" Not waiting for a reply she said,

"I'm disturbed by what I've seen and I'm not looking forward to the proceedings today,"

Storm searched her face with his eyes.

Rowena gave him a weak smile. "A sudden burst of energy to get me though the rest of the day would be welcome."

He clenched his teeth, reaching out to caress her cheek but was stopped by the look in her eyes. Instead, he stoked his hand down her arm. "I spoke with Albany. I ask him to withdraw his support for your involvement in these investigations. I see that sparks a bit of anger. I don't understand why you need to do this. You have no official standing in this mess."

"You have no right-"

"He told me the same. Actually he laughed and said you'd remove my manhood if you found out I was interfering in your quest."

She smiled as she understood what he was doing. "Your effort to revive me is appreciated. Damn, I don't even have the energy to argue."

"Doctor Rowena Radcliffe, lady of the manner, I'm shocked to hear something so course coming from your beautiful lips."

"Nothing shocks you. Besides, you're one of the few people in this city I know I can speak freely with who won't be offended."

"Is that a compliment? You've given me none in many years."

She studied his face, the powerful jaw, his dark shimmering eyes, the aristocratic nose, remembering a time when she'd thought he was meant only for her. He'd changed little over the years and it surprised her. She, on the other hand, had lost the bloom of youth.

This sudden yearning must be due to exhaustion.

Ignoring his questions she moved toward the door and changed the subject. "What brings you here? I can't imagine you have an abiding interest in the legal system and this is just an inquest." They walked together into the room where the proceeding was to be held.

"Attending one isn't the most interesting pursuit; however, you never know who may be present. You may be looking at the killer in this room, sitting on the sidelines in the guise of one of the reporters. Perhaps he's a causal observer, like me. Or, perhaps as you suggested, the killer may be that woman over there," he pointed across the room to a stout-looking woman seated beside a small, skeletal-looking man.

"You know I've made no such suggestion, only remarked a woman could have sufficient strength and fury to kill.

She saw the smirk on his lips but refused be baited further. She stepped around him and walked down the aisle to a seat near the wall in the back corner of the room.

"I must have said something outrageous. Normally you're so calm and cool, no matter what happens around you," he whispered with a grin and sat beside her, scooting close.

A stirring at the front drew their attention and made it difficult to continue the spat. Several of the officers involved in the investigation walked to the seats reserved for them. The only face she knew well was DI Abberline, though she'd met the other two men the night of the killing.

Shortly, Mr. Baxter, the coroner and his deputy, Mr. Collier, entered and took their respective seats. Calling the hearing open, they proceeded to spend a great deal of time seating the jury and addressing the coroner's complaint he didn't have a drawn plan of the murder site, even interrupting the testimony of Mr. Davis, the first to find Annie.

Mr. Davis was questioned on certain points then interrupted again.

"Constable, we must have that plan," Baxter instructed an officer sitting beside Abberline. "Go ahead Mr. Davis, finish what you were telling us."

As the day dragged on, it became clear there were no new revelations to be gained, nor had she really expected anything new. Most of the testimony by the witnesses related to verifying the identity of the deceased.

When the coroner finally adjourned for the day, Storm took her arm and pulled her out of the crowd exiting the room. "What if we call a truce? I know a little coffee house near here we can sit and talk."

She glanced toward her carriage, waiting at the curb, wondering how much longer she could deny how she felt about him.

"You can send Fagan home. I'll ensure you arrive home safely in time for your supper, unless you'd care to join me for dinner as well."

Before she could answer, she felt someone slam into her back. Turning she found herself looking into the hate-filled eyes of Morgana Ridley. Directly behind her was Bradley Sheffield, a secretive smile plastered across his face.

"Lady Radcliffe," he drawled. "You must forgive this stupid woman. She seems to have lost her balance for no apparent reason."

Instead of looking apologetic or the least bit uncomfortable, Morgana's face grew harder.

"We must make amends. You must join me down the street. There's a lovely new house that serves the most delicate coffees."

"She is not interested," de Grey growled, his lips curled back in disgust.

He looks like a dog preparing to attack.

"Garret, Bradley hasn't done anything offensive." She prayed she appeared friendly, as her stomach tightened.

Maybe he won't want to have Storm with us and will refuse.

"Surely, he can join if he wishes, Garret. Though I'm sure he needs to attend to...Morgana."

"She can wait in the carriage," Sheffield drawled carelessly shooing the nurse away. "She has that book she always carries as she mumbles her prayers. I'm sure it won't matter how long we have her wait."

Morgana's head whipped around, and her eyes seemed to stare into Sheffield's with a look of triumph for just the merest tick of the clock. Just as quickly she lowered her lids, staring down at the ground. A murmured "yes, my lord" could barely be heard above the noise of the still exiting crowd.

"So are we going to just stand here until someone else runs into us?" Sheffield quipped. "De Grey, why don't we ride along with you and I'll have my carriage follow. One of us can assure Lady Radcliffe a safe passage home later."

Storm's teeth clenched so hard, she wondered he didn't break them, but he refrained from saying what he so obviously thought as he guided her outside and into the carriage.

As they settled into the coach and it pulled away from the walk, Storm leaned forward into Sheffield's face. "You have more gall than any man I've ever met. I'm quite sure I saw you push that woman into Rowena."

"Why would I do such a thing? Doctor Radcliffe is a dear friend."

"I'm warning you Sheffield, if I

believe you even think about such a thing again, you'll answer to me."

Rowena grabbed Storm's arm and tried to pull him back. "This is preposterous. Why would Bradley do such a thing? Stop acting like this or I'll direct the driver to stop and call a public carriage to take me home."

Slowly de Grey sat back, but his eyes never left Sheffield's face. "You and that so-called nurse make an unholy union, Sheffield. I don't know what you're playing at, but I will find out."

The carriage rolled to a stop, and Sheffield leapt down offering his hand to Rowena, ignoring Storm completely. "Come, my dear, we can have a civilized bit of refreshment. You certainly don't believe the tale this hideous cretin is telling, now do you?"

"No. Of course not. Why would I ever imagine such a thing?" she replied as they stepped into the coffee house. It should have been a pleasurable reprise from the day spent listening to the details of death and friendship lost. The café was tolerably warm and the pungent aroma of fresh coffee filled the air. They were given a table in a quiet corner of the room. Rowena did her best to expel the tension.

Gossip and chit chat couldn't keep Storm from sitting in cold silence, eyes boring into Sheffield.

"Thank you gentlemen for a lovely and refreshing hour," she mocked. "I do however, believe I must return home."

"I will take you," Sheffield moved to take her arm. "I have to drive past your house."

"I will not let her get in that carriage alone with you," Storm proclaimed, his jaw tightening.

Sheffield smirked. "You forget Morgana is waiting. I'm sure she was content to read her bible as we sat and talked. It's a habit she's developed of late. I rarely see her without that ridiculous book. She's a perfectly acceptable companion to assure I do not despoil this sweet flower."

"Over my dead body."

"*Gentlemen.* And I use the term only because we're in public. I can make my own choice in this matter, and the choice I make will not be questioned." She looked from one to the other, waiting silently until their eyes were on her. "Lord de Grey, you offered your carriage earlier and I accepted."

Sheffield stuck out his lip and crossed his arms over his chest.

"Bradley remove that annoying pout from your face. It has been...never mind. Good night." Placing her hand firmly on de Grey's arm she allowed him to escort her to the carriage and assist her inside.

"Bloody hell and damnation, Storm, what was that?" she hissed as he stepped up and took his seat. "I've never been so embarrassed. You don't really think he pushed that woman into me do you?"

"I know he did Rowena, I saw him do it...and I saw the look of pleasure on her face as she hit you."

"Rubbish. You've always disliked Bradley, and you've gotten so much worse lately. You have to stop this."

For a moment she was sure he was going to curse her, instead he gritted his teeth, took a long deep breath and let it out slowly, sitting back.

Garret huffed. The tension eased from his shoulders. "Perhaps you're right. After dinner the other night, and everything else that's happened, I've come to distrust Sheffield more than usual. It's unholy the way those two seem to suddenly appear. However, I'm willing to accept I may overreact when he and that infernal woman are present. They set me on edge."

"It's a strange relationship to be

sure. I expected, when he decided to stay here in town, he'd immediately dismiss her."

"Do you think they are having an affair?" The idea seemed to perk Storm up.

"No. I hope not. I mean, can you even imagine it?" She snickered.

They looked at each other, both trying to suppress the laughter boiling up inside them, until it burst forth and filled the carriage just as it rolled to a stop outside Rowena's house. It had been a long time since they'd laughed so easily together.

"You could change your mind and go to dinner."

"We'll do that some other time. I really am tired and I just want a hot bath."

I don't want to spoil this bit of happiness between us. Dinner would just be an opportunity to destroy the mood.

"If that's what you want." She saw a wicked glint in his eyes. "I could assist you with that if you wish."

A smile crooked her lip. "Storm, please, we've been down that road and it's not one that takes us to any place good." She gave him a peck on the cheek as his driver lowered the step and offered her assistance exiting the carriage.

"We may be able to become friends again. I believe we've taken a few steps in the correct direction."

Hesitating, before stepping out, she turned to look at de Grey. "I'll think on it, but I am hesitant to say we are friends. I know how that can hurt should you decide to disappear again."

De Grey waved the driver away. "I never wanted to hurt you and I am here Row. Here to help you and protect you. You are in over your head and I don't want you harmed."

"I wouldn't even be here if it wasn't for you," she said the anger of years of hurt spewing out.

"What do you mean? What did I do?"

"You know what you did, Garrett de Grey. You refused to accept your responsibilities when your father died. You left me without a word."

"Rowena, I never meant...I can't-"

"I know. . You can't explain it. I waited Storm. I waited until I couldn't wait anymore then I went to America. That was a trip that set me on this road. Don't you dare tell me about how you fear for me or want to protect me. You lost that privilege a long time ago." She swung open the carriage door and stepped out unassisted. Why couldn't he have just stayed away? Left her to her life?

———

Morgana looked up from the book in her hand, "You said she would come with us. You told me I would have the opportunity to-"

"Shut up." Sheffield glared across the small aisle between them. "I didn't give you permission to speak. You're growing much too bold of late. Stick your nose back in that bloody book. If I hear another word from your mouth, I may have to take matters into hand and assure you understand your place."

Ignoring the warning she said, "I am the hand of the Lord God, I must teach others the error of their ways. The Lady's soul is in danger-"

His face contorted in anger. "This is not the game. You're nothing and you'll not ask me any questions nor speak your stupid thoughts. I grow tired of you."

She held her breath, biting at her lip until it bled.

"You don't want to end up like one of those vile whores do you? I'll personally throw you in the streets of Whitechapel if you irritate me again," he promised.

———

CHAPTER TWENTY

The papers were again full of the horror, presented in their usual *eloquent* manner. Of course, there was nothing subtle about the headlines. Frenzied reporters seemed to appear everywhere one looked. Today, in addition to the detailed reports, there was another story. A reward would be offered. The residents of Whitechapel had formed their own vigilance committee to patrol the streets and protect its residents.

Has anyone noticed not one respectable resident of Whitechapel has reported being approached by a crazed killer, and none of the victims are the staid housewives of these professional men?

Noting the time and place of the gathering Rowena tossed the paper aside. She wasn't a resident of the area, and held little regard for the men who were vowing to root out this killer, but she planned to attend their meeting.

———

The hall was crowded and everyone was talking at once. She heard the wildest speculation about the killer running like flood waters over the room. Most of the women present were huddled into one corner, a few were standing next to what she presumed to be their husbands, clinging to them and casting fearful glances as though expecting the killer to jump out at them from among the throng.

She worked her way toward the back corner away from the other women and took a seat at the end of the row. Few people paid her any attention until one of the reporters wandering about approached her.

"Lady Radcliffe. I'm surprised to find you in attendance."

"I can't think why you should be. I have an office in the area and am interested in what the committee will have to offer to those of us who are closer to the area where the investigation is being conducted."

"I wouldn't imagine they'll be running to your doorstep to help should you need it. It's my understanding they're interested only in the little plots of land that house them and their neighbors. I doubt they'd walk far enough down Whitechapel for a glance at the killer should he appear in the middle of the road during broad daylight with a sign pointing him out."

"You seem a bit cynical, mister-"

"Sorry, Randy Ball of the Sun. I saw you examining one of the victims. How is it you're allowed to get so close? I've never seen your name on any reports."

"So you didn't just walk over for a friendly chat. What is it you really want Mr. Ball?"

He smiled sheepishly. "A man's got to try to get an edge. Seems we're all reporting the same thing and it doesn't please my editor very much."

"Well, there's no story here. I did examine one of the unfortunate women, but there was nothing official."

"But you're a woman. Why would they allow you-"

"I'm also a doctor. I was returning from a late dinner when a lad running past our coach cried out a murder had been done. My escort, who has a...curiosity, directed his driver to the scene. One of the PC's knew me and thought I could help identify the woman. I do work with these unfortunates as I'm sure you know."

Ball looked at her with disbelief.

"I assure you, I didn't enjoy having to discard my newest frock and favorite shoes. Even if there hadn't been blood on them, the dirt from the streets of the area would have required me to throw them out."

She hoped he'd find her silly and perhaps a little arrogant, and end the discussion. Instead, he sat next to her as the crowd began to move toward their chairs in response to a speaker calling for silence.

She didn't recognize the man who was making the introductions, and the hum of the crowd made it difficult to hear what he said. He talked in a quiet tone of voice, perhaps a ruse to bring the room to silence. She was surprised to find it worked.

As the attendees quieted she heard the moderator say, "Mr. Lusk is an upstanding member of our community. He restores the buildings of our history. Works to keep our streets safe. He has been a solid presence during these horrible times, interviewing investigators and returning to us with accurate and relevant information about these slaughters. "

Lusk puffed out his chest as he stepped to the lectern. "I won't waste your time. We are living on the edge of a great and horrible danger. I and others here on the platform, are asking our neighbors to volunteer. We'll form a brigade to keep our wives and children safe."

"What can you do the constables and investigators aren't?" A man shouted from the center of the room.

"A fair question, Michael. We can patrol our streets at night. Add to the eyes already watching. At least two men will be assigned to guard our streets and alleyways, assuring no thief or killers lurk ready to strike. We can escort our women, and organize our servants so no female is left to walk alone on any errands."

"I have a business to run. How am I to stay up all night or be home all day to do this?" Another man, sitting in front of Rowena, called out.

Lusk frown at the man. "You've asked the question before, Pitney. We organize. We make sure different men do the patrols each night, so there is less loss of sleep for all. We ask for volunteers to be available during the day, and we ask the women to curb their outings, go in groups so it is easier to assure their safety."

"More like keep track of their activities," Ball whispered just loud enough for Rowena to hear.

Rowena hid her smile behind her gloved hand, and listened as more questions were called out. Lusk diligently worked to answer them all. Each time a response caused a buzz of conversation among those in attendance. He would stand tall, looking out on them and wait silently for the discussions to cease. She was surprised she found him so politically savvy, but she hated the things he said to raise the fear in the attendees.

Ball leaned closer. "Interesting man, he's done well for himself. I heard he came from humble beginnings and is now a pillar of the community. A bit pompous though."

She didn't want to like the young reporter, but he said exactly what she had been thinking. Had he not been a newsman, she might have invited him to tea some time. Still might at some time in the future.

The meeting droned on as she

scanned the room to see the reactions of the people. Glimpsing a woman's face on the other side of the room, she wondered briefly if it was Morgana, but she didn't have to opportunity to get a better look as the meeting erupted into a shouting match. Reporters, who had been ignored, stood and began to shout out their questions. Deciding this was the opportune moment, she slipped out of her seat and through the back door of the hall, where she almost collided with de Grey.

Bloody hell. "I didn't notice you inside. What are you doing here?"

"I might ask the same of you."

"I'm on my way home." She stepped to the side continuing toward her carriage.

His hand snaked out as she tried to pass. Grabbing her arm, he spun her back toward him. "Rowena, I've tried to be nice. I've spent a great deal of effort avoiding a confrontation with you, but you have to stop your excursions into these streets at night. Even a meeting such as this is not safe. You need protection."

"I've been independent for a long time, de Grey. I've lived on my own and done as I pleased. You can't dictate what I shall and shall not do. Donald has made it clear you're a part of this investigation, though I don't understand what you have to offer. I've been civil and even friendly, to a point, but don't stand in my way." She stepped back, and rubbed her arm where he had grabbed her.

"Row...I-"

"*Don't* call me that," she hissed through her teeth as others from the meeting began to pour out of the building. "We've been through this before. That was a name of affection, and the affection died long ago. Nothing you've done has given you the right to try to soften me with memories of the past."

Something behind her had distracted him, and he didn't answer. Turning she stepped away again, a curt good night on her lips, but when she looked back where he'd stood, he'd disappeared.

——

CHAPTER TWENTY-ONE

She hadn't slept well. The exaggerated warnings of danger given by Lusk and his cronies rang through her head for a good part of the night. When she did manage to fall asleep, it was to see Storm de Grey. She could feel the warmth of him as though his arms were wrapped around her. She could feel the touch of his lips to hers. There were so many things about him she remembered as she relived the memories she'd tried so hard to forget. Giving up she tossed on her robe.

Daylight was just beginning to peek over the horizon and it would be some time before her normal breakfast hour. She fixed herself a pot of tea and took it into the garden to watch the rising sun. Clouds edged in gold drifted lazily across the horizon. As the sun rose higher hot pink streaks brightened the sky. The lyrical songs of birds filled the air as they awakened. Jasmine, rose, and lavender scents spiced the morning air. It would be a glorious day.

Sipping from the delicate cup, she admitted she had to address the difficulties caused by having Storm back in her life. There was a time she had loved him but that was over. Wasn't it? He'd gambled. Refused to act responsibly. Was seen in the company of ruffians. Then she'd discovered he'd been planning to leave. Before she could question him he had disappeared. Flight from the heartbreak he caused had set her on her current path. She'd gone to America to visit a cousin and met Doctor Elizabeth Blackwell.

Dr. Blackwell was an amazing woman, who had tricked the stuffy and staid medical college into admitting her to their hallowed halls. Receiving her medical degree she had found it hard to open a practice until the Civil War had taken its toll and she was needed to care for the mangled and dying solders.

Returning home from the war Elizabeth Blackwell had opened her own medical school for woman, thumbing her nose at the men who had wanted so desperately to expel her from their midst. The unique woman had been the answer to forgetting Storm de Grey and had given Rowena a way of extracting revenge on the pompous medical men who treated her like an ignorant child as her mother lay dying.

———

Studying the letter she'd received from Thomas Bond, she read the missive for the third time, absorbing his projected image of the killer.

> *I'm certain the man is misogynistic. His hatred of women is displayed in the selection of the prostitutes as the focus for his fury during the attacks. He will set himself apart from society and have few friends and no stable occupation. I further believe he may be suffering from Satyriasis, an uncontrollable desire to perform the sexual act. This belief has*

basis in the probability he has used these women for his own pleasure at some time, or even immediately before he attacks them. He believes they are the cause of his desperate immoral need to possess them.

Indeed, Thomas you could be correct, but I can't agree. Although there is still much to be learned. My studies of the men who kill in this manner indicate if they become frenzied they cannot suddenly stop. They must complete their goal and have no restraint.

Though the actions of the killer could support the theory some sexual deviancy was present in these killings, she believed the wounds were intentional. Deliberate. Not the frenzied slashing that appeared on the rest of the torso. The other areas were torn and ragged, but this didn't seem to be the case where the organs had been removed. Why had the killer suddenly altered his behavior? What could have made him calm down and take such care?

She'd been very thorough in her examinations, compared the location of the wounds on all the women they suspected had been murdered by this fiend. Was it possible there was some ritual being performed?

However, she had to agree with Bond's evaluation of the occupation of the killer. This person must not be stable enough to hold down a position of any responsibility. It was one of the reasons she didn't give regard to the suspects being touted as a certainty by the newspapers, a butcher, a doctor, and a sailor among them.

Some of the experts firmly declared only a professional man could have removed the organs. But most of these experts were stuffy old men who had little experience with more than the wife beater who broke a bottle and used it to slash his wife.

Neither she nor Bond believed the killer was skilled in surgery nor was he a professional butcher as some claimed. The incisions at the neck and abdomen were not as precise as one might expect from such professionals. There was an indication they were started and stopped more than once before they were completed. The initial cut might cause sufficient bleeding to severely disable or kill the victim but they were incomplete compared to the result. Was it possible they were intentionally cut in this manner to keep them from calling out?

She had to understand this killer. Was driven to understand. Not just the killer's mind, but the patterns that could be found at the scenes. The threads that would help determine the type of person capable of such horrendous acts. Yet to date the information she'd gathered could well send the police in too many directions, confuse the investigators and allow a killer to go free. If she failed, she'd never be able to live with the results.

Shaking her head, she poured more tea into her empty cup and returned to her review of the letter. Bond's words were disturbing and she wanted to be sure she hadn't misread or misinterpreted them.

> *As to your friend Bradley Sheffield, I do have grave concerns about his nature. He lacks boundaries that a civilized man would accept and expect. He appears narcissistic in the extreme.*

His heritage and upbringing do not explain this trait. Men of his station are trained to control themselves.

Based on your description of Lord Sheffield's action he is trying to manipulate and intimidate those around him regardless of their station in life. He has displayed this tactic frequently by arriving at your surgery uninvited and stating his expectation he would be welcomed. He expects you to allow him to take your arm and lead you about even without your permission. And more disturbing is the callous treatment you described of his servants, especially Morgana Ridley.

Finally, I find his sense of what he believes to be fun strange to the point I might worry he could well overstep the bounds of society.

Thomas's letter added to her unease. She felt as though she must tread lightly around Sheffield. A feeling she had never felt before. She had known Bradley Sheffield since they'd been children. They had shared the same parties and disciplines. Her father had mourned for weeks when Lord Sheffield had died unexpectedly and had offered Bradley help with the duties of his estate.

She didn't want to believe the boy she'd known might have become a monster, but was afraid he might well be walking down that dark path at this very time in his life.

———

"My lady, Lord Sheffield is in the library and asked if you'll permit him to attend you," Günter announced.

Rowena closed her eyes, schooling her face to remain neutral. Just as the letter had stated, Sheffield had lost all sense of boundaries. "Tell him I'll be with him shortly," she said as she slipped Bond's letter into the drawer with the other materials she had relating to the crimes.

"Bradley, I told Gunter I would come to you when I was done. What brings you here?" Rowena asked as he entered the room, angry he had refused to wait.

"I haven't seen you since the

funeral. Wasn't it a bit maudlin? Morgana insisted she must attend and I thought it might break the boredom I have been experiencing. After all there's so much chatter in the press these days."

The funeral was maudlin? What had he expected? He hadn't made her uncomfortable until recently but now she grew more wary every time they met. Today the look on his face sent a chill slithering down her spine. For just a moment, as he walked toward her, she feared he would try to give her a peck on the cheek. The thought turned her stomach. She was thankful when he made no such attempt.

"I've been following the stories in the news. Of course that made me think of you. You have such interesting ideas. Access to all the most secret tidbits. I was hoping you would share a few about the killer since you won't allow me those gruesome little reports."

"I have nothing to share." It took all the discipline of her training to keep from rubbing at the chills that crept up her arms. "Other than the details of the coroner's inquests, reported accurately in the papers, I don't know anything more than the average reader."

"Darling, I know you're telling just a little fib. Besides, there must be more, with all the speculation in the news."

"I think the news stories are just journalistic sensationalism. The imagination of the reporters and their editors is running rampant. It seems to me every third man on the streets of Whitechapel is accused of being the killer."

"That's *precisely* what I mean. Rowena, you always say exactly what you think," he laughed as he stepped to the sideboard and helped himself to a glass of whiskey uninvited. "It's been over two weeks since the last killing and every day I read of another arrest, or reported suspicion. It's all quite delightful."

"Bradley. I believe you're becoming more callous by the moment. False accusations can ruin the lives of those men and aren't a matter to be taken lightly. So many of the reports are based on prejudice and fear of others without basis."

"Forgive me, I didn't mean to scoff at something you believe is unrighteous. I really came by to invite you to dinner one evening. I believe I owe you and the other guests you had at your table."

"I'm sure none of us feels you owe us such an invitation. I know my schedule is quite full as I am sure are de Grey's and Swanson's. However if it can be arranged I will try to attend."

"Wonderful." He set the empty glass aside. "Then I'll send my man around with the date and time. Take care. Oh, and Rowena, I hear you are still making your little sojourns into those dark and dangerous streets. I'd not like to see anything happen to you because of your interests. Sometimes it's not healthy to dig too deeply into the mind of a killer."

Rowena didn't know how to respond so remained silent.

"Goodness, I do sound so serious," he laughed as he waved good-bye and walked out the door.

Disgust snaked along her nerves. She stepped to the doorway and watched him saunter down the stairs. Feeling slightly ill she wondered how far he'd gone into the dark world which seemed to fascinate him so, and how far he was willing to descend. Every sense screamed she should take care to avoid being alone with the man again.

———

The voyeur waited until two women came out of the pub laughing as they were joined by paying clients. Furtively stepping back into the shadows to let them pass, the monster tread lightly after them. It was always such fun to observe the whores ply their trade in the alleys and dark doorways. They could be so inventive in the way they made themselves available to the men.

But tonight was different. This time the subject of focus left her friend to ply her trade in a stairwell, then clung to her own client, led him into the rooms where she was staying. The house was dark, no lights showing as they approached.

It was frustrating not to be able to follow. Starting to walk away, the watcher stopped, turning to look down the shadow-filled alley that ran along the building. Light suddenly escaped from a narrow window that had been dark. Cautiously looking around, wanting to assure no one was in the street to observe, the voyeur gazed into the room through the uncovered glass.

She was there. She and her sailor struggling to undress, stumbling and laughing drunkenly. Her *client* slipped a small bottle of liquor from his trousers, passing it to her as he began to unbutton them. Drinking and tripping over each other they finally fell onto the bed partially dressed. *What a perfect place to die*, he thought enjoying the antics until the couple fell into a drunken stupor.

———

De Grey followed Rowena and Sheffield into the dining room, a scowl on his face seen only by Swanson. They were seated and served in silence. They had agreed not to discuss the murders during the meal but no one seemed able to make pleasant conversation though Bradley tried. As the courses were served and removed, those present played at eating. Finally he invited them to retire to the library where sherry for Rowena and drinks for the men had already been poured and set out for them.

Rowena took a seat beside Sheffield's desk, slightly away from the others. Glancing at the blotter he used to write notes, a laugh escaped her when she saw the familiar red ink stains. She'd always found it childish, the way he corresponded in colored ink when he was upset. But this bit of unexpected normalcy helped her to relax for a moment as she asked, "Who are you chastising now?"

"No one special. You have to admit I do get my point across to those who receive my notes."

She smirked. "So, we've heard nothing further from the killer? Do you think he's left the area?"

Donald Swanson bit down on his pipe and shifted in his chair, but made no response.

Storm pointedly looked at each of them before making a gruff reply. "Sheffield, I don't understand your interest. These killings are not your usual fare. Why are you interested in these pathetic women?"

"You can't pick up a paper and not be inundated with the story. You can't escape from it even as you walk down the street. You hear about it everywhere, the story is on the lips of every person you meet."

"So, that explains your interest, and our invitation to dinner tonight?"

"Of course. I'm close to the source of the investigation. You're all *friends*. Why shouldn't I tap your knowledge to make me more interesting at the card salons? I need some fun and this inactivity by the killer is tiresome."

Sheffield and de Grey would never be friends, but tonight their differences created an intolerable atmosphere.

"I for one don't wish to play this

game. If you'll excuse me." Storm set his whiskey aside as he rose. "Lady Radcliffe, Swanson, I believe I'll retire for the evening." de Grey said ignoring their host as he strode quickly from the room.

Donald looked uncomfortable, as though he too wished to rush away.

Rowena turned her attention back to Sheffield, anxious to escape but trying to smooth over the abrupt departure. She hoped to keep Bradley from saying something he might regret in front of Swanson.

"I believe we're all on edge, waiting to see what happens next. I admit I am losing sleep wondering if there will be a knock at the door. I did not realize how tired I was. Forgive me, but I think I must beg your leave as well. I'll ask Donald to escort me out to my carriage if you don't object."

"*Go.* I find your company irritating," Sheffield dismissed them with a wave of his hand.

Rowena could see the vein throbbing in his neck. He didn't even bother to rise and make his good-byes, but she was relieved he hadn't tried to stop them.

As they gathered their coats and

hats, Rowena noticed Morgana hovering in an unlit doorway. Averting her eyes, she acted as though she hadn't seen the woman and stepped out on the stoop with Swanson.

"Thank you, my lady," Swanson said as he set his hat on his head. "I wasn't sure how to make my excuses and I didn't wish to leave you there alone."

"Oh."

He laughed when she raised a brow. "You were intent on rescuing me."

It was the first smile she'd seen on his face the entire evening. "You don't have to accept these invitations, Donald. I know you're very busy directing the investigations, and you take an active part in the work being done."

"Your friend de Grey is right though. I admit I'm uneasy. I keep waiting for the knock on my door announcing another murder, so I hardly sleep. I was certainly not at my best over dinner."

"I believe we all share the same discomfort." She accepted his assistance as she stepped into her carriage. "I hope your unease is for naught, though I fear we'll hear from our villain again soon." As the carriage rolled away from the curb, she prayed her words would not come true.

CHAPTER TWENTY-TWO

"I don't know what this means. It may not be anything, but I wanted your opinion. I'm drawing a blank. This damnable case is wearing on me."

She sat quietly across the desk from Donald Swanson as he prepared to read her the copy of the letter received by the Central News.

"Even the first line is outrageous. I don't have the words to express my disgust. It begins-

"Dear Boss,

> *I keep on hearing the police have caught me but they wont fix me just yet. I have laughed when they look so cleaver and talk about being on the right track."*

270

It's as though he wants us to believe he's in our very midst, listening to our conversations." He crumpled the paper as his hands fisted.

Rowena reached over and gently retrieved the pages, quickly scanning the rest of the message. "Is this an exact copy? I mean no changes in the spelling or words?"

"Yes. You think the words have some significance, other than what they say of course?"

Rowena glanced at the paper. "Give me a moment to read though it a few times."

That joke about Leather apron gave me real fits. I am down on whores and I shant quit ripping them till I do get buckled. Grand work the last job was, I gave the lady no time to squeal. How can they catch me now I love my work and want to start again. You will soon hear of me with my funny little games. I saved some of the proper red stuff in a ginger beer bottle over the last job to write with but it went thick like glue and I cant use it. Red ink is fit enough I hope ha. ha. The next job I do I shall clip the ladys ears off and send to the police officers just for jolly wouldn't you. Keep this letter back till I do a bit more work then give it out straight. My knife's so nice and sharp I want to get to work right away if I get a change, good luck.

Yours truly
Jack the Ripper.

Don't mind me giving the trade name.

Wasn't good enough to post before this I got all the red ink off my hands curse it. No luck yet. They say I'm a doctor now. Ha ha

"It's interesting he named himself," Rowena said noting that Swanson was looking quite anxious.

"What is your opinion?"

Rowena glanced back down at the copy she held in her hand, "I feel he strives to sound somewhat illiterate in his wording,

272

but some of the words used seem to indicate he's well schooled. For example the sentence containing the words, *will soon hear of me with my funny little games* certainly doesn't appear to be written by some unschooled fellow. Of course I don't really know much about analyzing what has been written."

Rowena watched as Swanson muttered then clamped down on the stem of his pipe, chewing the stem in an action that appeared unconscious.

Shaking his head as if to clear his thoughts he said, "Whoever he is he has to be getting quite a laugh out of this."

"Do you think it was really written by the killer?"

"We've sent the original to our experts. They'll make a complete analysis and come to no conclusion. However, personally I'd wager it's some reporter wishing to keep the readers buying his paper. Most of the news mongers seem disappointed we've not had another slaughter."

"I'd agree. In my opinion the killer would have included some detail not reported, though there are few. He'd wish to make sure you knew it was really him."

"*Exactly*. Excuse me a moment."

Donald waved to his assistant and called out for tea. "I feel a bit parched."

"How are you and your investigators faring? I've read there have been a number of accusations and arrests. I note most of these have resulted in releases. It must be difficult to know who to believe with everyone so frightened and turning on their neighbors."

Swanson bit down hard on the stem of his unlit pipe, before setting it aside. "You can't imagine. Yesterday we had a man confess. Claimed his wife, a gypsy witch, cast a spell on him. Turns out he isn't married and wasn't even in town when the Nichols murder occurred. Of course we didn't discover this for some time, spent hours talking as he listed the details of what he'd done. I wish the blasted, excuse me My Lady, news rags would be more selective in their reports."

"Everyone knows too many of the details from the news reports of the inquests. It makes it much harder to determine who is a liar and who is sincere."

Swanson sighed and rested his head on the back of his chair before straightening, then reached for his pipe and tobacco. He struck a match and before placing it to the bowl he waited for Rowena to give him permission to smoke as Thompson arrived with the tea. "Thank you for coming, my lady. I'm afraid I've taken advantage of our acquaintance, but I feel I can speak openly in your presence. I admit that's not something I permit myself to do with most."

"I'm flattered you feel that way. You're in a very difficult position and I'm sure the Home Office as well as the reporters and citizenry are pressuring you. You know you can trust Storm...Lord de Grey, as well." *Though I hate to admit it.*

"Yes, I do. May I be so bold as to ask how he came by that name?"

Rowena laughed politely. "Sorry the name just seems to slip out of late. Garrett is known for his temper. You can almost see the storm clouds gathering when he's upset. When he strikes at the target of his ire, it's like a bolt of lightning striking them down."

"He's violent?"

"No, of course not," she chuckled "not at all. He's a master of cutting a man in half using only his silver tongue. When he speaks you hear the roar of thunder, thus the name Storm."

The sound of someone clearing their throat had Rowena turning to look at the doorway. She hadn't seen him since the night of Sheffield's disastrous dinner party.

Damnation, can I go nowhere without you following behind? Even as she thought the words she felt her heart do a flip at the sight of him.

"Lord de Grey," Swanson said, his face turning a dark pink. "I didn't expect you this afternoon. Come in, we were discussing the letter sent over by the News."

"So I heard."

The pink darkened to a bright red on Donald's cheeks, but Rowena noted the humor in Storm's eyes.

"Yes...well...umm..."

"I take no offense. Actually, I like my sobriquet. It goes well with my surname and fits my temperament. May I see the letter?"

Rowena handed de Grey the papers. "Donald has forwarded the original off for evaluation." She stiffened as he reached toward her.

Hell, why did he have to catch me speaking lightly of him? He'll think...who cares what he thinks.

"So, do you believe this is actually from our villain?"

As Swanson was still recovering from his embarrassment, Rowena responded, "We think perhaps it's more likely to have come from the pen of one of the reporters. Second choice would be some jokester playing a hoax."

"Plausible. It's been quiet for the greater part of three weeks. I'd suppose sale of the news has decreased, though they continue to cover the inquests although there has been nothing new there. It makes sense someone would try to stir the pot."

De Grey's lip quirked as he handed the papers across the desk to the Chief Inspector. "So, what did you think of Sheffield's little dinner party? I heard you mention him as I stood in the door. I personally find his interest in the murders somewhat morbid, thus my quick exit."

The question seemed to cause Donald more discomfort than had the earlier discussion. "Storm, you shock our host. You're aware he has superiors to report to and can't be overheard making comments about Sheffield or anyone else for that matter."

"Oh, you can speak freely with me. I personally find the man repulsive. I only agreed to attend to assure Rowena would not be alone with him and that tedious woman he calls a nurse."

Donald snorted, then quickly tried to compose himself.

"See Row, he agrees. There is something very wrong with those two individuals." He turned to look straight at Swanson. "Perhaps they should be investigated. I'm sure you could arrest them for impersonating humans, at the very least."

"Lord de Grey." Swanson, eyes wide, shot a glance at the open door where his assistant sat, pretending not to listen.

Rowena slapped at de Grey's hand. "Why are you so intent on being difficult today? Someone could overhear this conversation and cause Donald a great deal of trouble."

"Nonsense, I wouldn't leave his feet dangling over the coals. Sorry Inspector, as I said Sheffield is disgusting and I find it difficult to speak civilly about him. Rowena, you were the first to tell me he has a darker nature. How is it you still call yourself his friend?"

"Not friend. It's difficult to explain. Though I admit lately he seems...more cavalier and callous. It was an uncomfortable evening. Did you notice the woman? She was lurking in the hallway while we dined."

Swanson cleared his throat, and glanced at the door again nervously.

"Yes, and later she was barely hidden inside the door to the library. Not very effective at concealing herself." Storm stood and closed the office door. "Or perhaps she had no interest in concealing herself. Wanted us to know she was about."

"What an odd way to think. You believe she was really wanted to be discovered?" Rowena asked.

"Yes and you must wonder why," Storm reclaimed his chair. "Now we don't have to worry someone will hear everything we say. So tell me how the investigation is really going."

"Not well, not well at all." Swanson tapped his pipe against his foot and reached for the tobacco. "What little we have in the way of witnesses...well everyone disagrees as you know. There has been nothing left at the site of the murders that is unusual or telling. No one knows of any specific person or persons who have been near the area and appeared to exhibit any unusual behavior. But in that part of London those who might notice would never tell us.

Rowena took a sip of the cooled tea, shaking her head to indicate she didn't want Swanson to call for a fresh pot. "Is there a way to track the person who mailed the letter? I know it probably won't lead to the killer, but-"

"A waste of time and resources," de Grey responded for the Inspector. "My men have had no luck either."

"Your men?"

"Swanson and Anderson, with the blessings of Albany, have accepted my help. I'm sure you remember the rabble I was drinking with when you were returning to town. They offered their assistance as well, and have been living and working in the area. None of them have been any more successful than the investigators and constables."

"Why am I just now hearing about this?"

"There was no need to tell you," Swanson replied. "The fewer people aware of this tactic, the less chance there is to let the information slip out."

"You think I would let something *slip out*? So why are you telling me this now?"

"Lord de Grey is concerned for your safety. One or the other of the men will be about when you are holding your surgery days. We don't wish you to be alarmed should you notice them."

Rowena sat back in the chair, silently listing the reasons she shouldn't get up and walk out of the room after telling these men what she thought of their concerns.

"Row...Rowena, I don't want to upset you, nor do we want to do anything to hinder your ability to provide care to the people you so fervently wish to help. The men won't be obvious. They will look and act like any of the men who live and work along those streets. You knew of my concerns, and when Swanson and I visited several days ago, I told him how much I am bothered by the fact the two women who died recently have been under your care."

"His concerns aren't outrageous, and he didn't make any demands or indicate he would do this on his own. I, too, fear this is not a sad coincidence. When you deal with those who are willing to kill, when the killing is not a spontaneous act of passion, there can be something...somewhere they look for their victims."

"I can agree with this conclusion, my studies support such a possibility and I determined this might be a factor at the last scene of crime. I also see no argument I might make will change your minds. Will I at least know who to look for, in case I should notice someone you haven't placed outside my door?"

"Yes, we're meeting tomorrow afternoon here in the Inspector's office. If you should care to join us briefly, perhaps drop by to retrieve your gloves, I'll be glad to introduce you to some of the men," de Grey offered.

"I had no idea you were so interested in covert missions, Storm." It was hard to keep the sarcasm out of her voice. "I admit I'm surprised you've taken this on. I'd begun to believe you were just one more aristocrat bent on wasting his life away. I'll have to adjust to this side of your nature."

"Then it's settled. Lady Radcliffe. De Grey, it's been an interesting and productive afternoon," Swanson said, the desire to move them on their way written clearly on his face. "Now, I've a report to prepare for my superiors. We'll soon meet again."

As they left the room, Storm's lips quirked into a half smile. "I believe he dismissed us rather well. He appears to some to be a bit weak, but I think he's well in charge of himself and others. Have you forgiven me yet, for all this?"

"For once again interfering in my life? Directing what I do? No. I won't forgive you. However, I'm no fool, Garret. I understand as I told you both in Donald's office, but I don't like it. I never will."

———

CHAPTER TWENTY-THREE

She couldn't help but wonder if Swanson realized how prophetic his words had been as she and de Grey left his office. They would meet again too soon. She'd only been to bed a few hours when the dreaded knocking sounded at her door.

From the window of her carriage she watched as Donald hurriedly stepped from the scene of crime into his own coach which immediately pulled away. There was no need to guess where he was going. They would see each other again this night. Much too soon.

In the alley she carefully stepped

around the blood pooled about the victim. She breathed slowly, waiting until she could adjust to the smell of death that hung about the scene. Hiking her skirt just enough to keep it dry, she lowered herself next to the woman, examining the face and destruction the killer had left behind. She tried to block out thoughts of the next woman she would go to examine. Two victims in one night. The rumors flying through the air threatened to distract her.

This one, if any victim of violent death could be, was lucky. Only her throat had been slashed and one might think someone other than the specific killer they sought had slain her. But Rowena felt the same dark feeling she'd experienced before at all the other scenes. It permeated the air, thick with evil.

She thought the woman was called Long Liz, though she'd only seen her once when she'd needed treatment for a nasty burn on her arm. Flat Bitsy had brought her in at the recommendation of Mary Kelly. Of course she couldn't be sure, and ultimately it would be for the police to ascertain her name. Find any loved ones, tell them the tragic news.

A flash of anger sped through her. These women all had someone who'd cared. Her heart still twisted with grief at the thought of Annie Chapman, a woman who drank too much but worked and tried to make a better life for herself and the man she loved. She had a family who'd mourn her for the rest of their lives. Why would anyone think they had the right to take so much away from so many?

"Rowena...Row?"

She glanced through tear-blurred eyes at the highly polished shoes beside her. She blinked and slowly scanned up the long legs, the hand, reaching out to offer assistance, the powerful arms and broad shoulders, then to the finely chiseled face.

He has the solidity of an oak tree and the bearing of a royal. Why haven't I noticed the change in him before? This isn't the irresponsible boy I believed him to be. Here, even with the subject of the brutal attack lying at her feet, she yearned to have him take her in his arms and shield her from the deadly night.

He bent down to take her arm, help her stand beside him.

"No, I haven't finished my exam," she said but failed to resist as he helped her rise.

"You've seen enough of this one.

Come. I'll take you to the next."

He pushed a way for them through the growing crowd, cutting a path to where his carriage stood waiting. They rode silently.

She prepared to make one more hideous venture into the night. Prepared to see pools of blood glistening in the flickering lamp light of the constables. To witness the senseless waste of a life. She needed to find the steel within herself to remain cool and calm when what she really wanted to do was run screaming into the darkness.

As the coach started its journey to the next victim, Rowena balled her hand into a fist. Her nails cut into the palm of her hand until she was sure it would bleed. *Don't show them how hard this is. Don't show any weakness. They will claim they are right. They will claim a woman should not be permitted here.*

She took a deep breath to steady herself as the coach stopped.

"Row, you don't, I repeat, don't have to do this. You're under no legal or ethical obligation. You asked to study. To learn. To understand. But you've seen enough. I know Albany would never have said yes if he could see what it's costing you."

"You can't stop me, Storm. Not by calling me a tender name from the past, nor pleading, nor making demands. This is something I'm driven to do. I have to find a way to translate what's done to the victim to help catch a killer. Put him away where he can never harm anyone again."

"I thought you wanted to understand the killers, help them find their way out of the abyss."

"I don't believe anyone can. How can a normal person understand someone, something like this, so foreign? How can we reach out to them and make them feel our distress at their actions? This rogue is like a snake. A snake that demonstrates no emotion. Only has an awareness of its own needs."

"You think that is the kind of person who's capable of this carnage?"

The carriage bumped across a hole in the road and they suddenly found themselves swaying from side to side for a moment.

Rowena reached for the strap at the side of the carriage door to steady herself. "Yes, and I believe there are things common to certain types of killers.

However some scientists don't believe as I do. When I was in North America studying, there was a lecture by a horrible little man who extolled the fallacy of such a concept. But as I learned from those already in captivity I began to believe Dr. Bond's and Dr. Phillips' theories were correct. I wrote to them in support and that's how I became friends with Thomas. I am certain when we find this fiend we will be able to reap further proof they are correct."

"But you've spent your entire life trying to care for others, not track down killers. You became a doctor to *help* people. I thought I understood you but find we actually stand on opposite ends of the earth. I never understood your need to help everyone you met. More I don't understand this need to find a killer. Will I ever understand you, Row?"

"I don't know. But recognizing your confusion makes me feel a bit closer to you. Makes me want you...as my friend. It's more than we ended with."

De Grey looked out the window, taking note of the growing crowd. "We'll have to finish this later. Are you ready to face this one?"

Taking a deep breath, she nodded. She held his hand tightly as she stepped from the coach.

They approached together in the dark. The lamps around the square weren't working properly. Storm took a lantern from one of the constables they encountered as they walked to where the figure lay, legs splayed, her abdomen a gaping wound. Most of the constables were spread across the yard, as distant from the woman as they dared to be. Although the face had been attacked, Rowena felt sure she was looking at Catherine Eddowes. She fought to keep from crying out as she recognized the design under the blood on the dress the woman was wearing. Catherine was another of the women to first give her a chance, to show a little trust and allow her to provide medical treatment.

"De Grey, my lady." Swanson came toward them, holding his arms out as if to block their approach. "You'll have to speak with Inspector Collard before you examine this one. She belongs to the City Police as she died only a few steps from our authority. I'm sure he'll cooperate, but again, you'll have to do as he asks."

"I'll take care of this," Storm said, walking over to the man Donald had pointed out.

"You were at Dutfield's Yard when I left. Do you think it was the same killer?"

She nodded, glancing over at Catherine, wishing she could do...something. "Yes. Perhaps he was interrupted, or warned away as a constable approached so didn't complete the task on the first, but I believe it is the same madman."

Storm returned. "Collard's agreed to let you take a look, but none of us will be reported in the official documents. He has the same fears Anderson expressed, and wants no one to think Scotland Yard is taking over the case, though he's sure you'll receive official notification by wire, he said to Swanson."

Rowena noticed Swanson didn't find it surprising he wasn't welcome by the city police. And she'd been prepared to have them treat her as some aberrant anomaly and strike all knowledge of her from their memories. "I have no difficulty accepting the terms. However it's a shame I can't give an official statement naming her. She was one of mine as well. If I'm correct in the identification of the woman at Dutfield's you'll discover she also attended my surgery in the past few months."

"So it's all linked, but what-"

"Please, not here. I can't...the responsibility weighs too heavily upon me. How can four murders on these streets, populated by so many I do not know, all come back to me?"

The two men didn't answer as Collard called out for Rowena.

"So you're the lady doctor, huh?" Collard had a sneer plastered across his face.

"You know I am," Rowena replied, her voice sweet as honey.

"So, Swanson seems to think you're somethin' special. I think you know a lot more about these murders than you been tellin' him and his fancy Metropolitan crew. I heard you been following this monster from Germany."

Rowena couldn't believe what he seemed to be implying.

Storm stepped in front of her before she could answer. "Man, are you trying to accuse Lady Radcliffe of being involved in this horror? I'll have your head for this."

Collard coughed, taking a step back. "I didn't mean...I just-"

"You apologize this instant or I promise you will regret it."

"Storm, the detective is right to question me." She took his arm, gently pulling him away from the detective. "I'm surprised it has taken so long for someone to do so, but I am not offended. Leave the man alone."

"Row, he—"

"He is asking the questions no one else has. Inspector, I can assure you I don't know who is responsible for these horrors, but I pray you or the Metropolitan learn the answer to that soon."

"Well. Um. Yes. I didn't mean no offense, my lady. I just_"

"I understand so can we proceed with the viewing of the body?"

Collard stepped aside to let Rowena and de Grey pass.

Catherine, often called Kate by her friends, fared far worse than the woman at Dutfields. Rowena looked at the disfigured face. If she hadn't known Kate so well, and spoken with her only the day before, she wasn't sure she'd have recognized her.

The person who had done this was past insane. The attack had been brutal, more so than any of the others.

The attack on the face is personal, meant to degrade. Something is driving the killer to a higher stage of rage. Was the killer trying to destroy the identity of the victim or did he perceive the prey was

293

looking at him, taunting him from the dark side of death?

They had to find the killer soon.

———

CHAPTER TWENTY-FOUR

Swanson and de Grey were expected at any moment. Rowena had offered her study for their meeting. It was comfortable, and there would be no gossips to hear their conversation. Her servants were loyal and very discreet. Margaret brought in the tea and cakes, disappearing quickly and quietly when everything was laid out.

Donald Swanson was visibly upset as he came in and sat down. "I suppose you saw the posting, a second letter...a postcard actually, delivered to Central News again. We've taken it over for evaluation."

"Do you think it's from the same person?"

"It referred to a double event, but everyone knew of the two killings this morning and we can't determine when it was posted. Then there is the fact the public is well versed on the first letter, since it was published in every newspaper on seven continents. Everyone in the world knew about the offer to send us a part of the ear, which of course he hasn't. I still believe it's someone from the paper. Just a bit convenient and I wonder no postal clerk has stepped forward to tell us he read the communication during the process of receiving it or delivering the bloody thing."

Storm, who'd arrived while Swanson was speaking, poured them both a stout glass of whiskey before sitting down. "Still no viable suspects? What are you going to do now?"

"There's an attempt to use bloodhounds if there is another killing. A waste of time in my opinion. They are to do some trials at Regent's and Hyde Parks today and tomorrow. I can't imagine they'll be very effective. I know they're tracking dogs, but the crowds are growing larger at every funeral and every killing. How will the dogs be able to track through all of that?"

Rowena shook her head. "I'd planned to go to the Eddowes' funeral yesterday, but was called to an emergency. I noticed the news had sketches of purported suspects. I have to admit they look like just about every second man I meet. One even looks a bit like that George Lusk."

Swanson and de Grey nodded their heads in agreement.

"My inspectors are overwhelmed with suspects," Swanson said. "It's becoming more outrageous by the moment. Every man who owns a knife has been reported as this *ripper*. There are even rumors the royals are involved and the police are covering up for their criminal activities. I have to admit I've rarely felt so much pressure. Sir Warren is bearing the brunt of it, of course. As Chief Commissioner he has to deal with the Home Office, the Mayor, and even members of the parliament. I don't envy him."

De Grey, who knew Sir Charles and had little care for him, shrugged. "A pity. So how is the London police investigation going?"

"I have copies of their reports and those from the coroner. Nothing we haven't heard before. They do seem to have an agreement of sorts between two witnesses who saw two men at two separate times, but Inspector McWilliams is not being very forthright in offering us all the information he has. Fortunately I have friends on the force who like to share," the Chief Inspector said with a conspiratorial smile.

"So is there anything we don't already know?" Garret asked.

"As I said there's a description which seems consistent in two separate sightings, but again it is somewhat general. A man, maybe two, one a gentlemen wearing his best dress, the only things the two witnesses seemed to agree on was at least one man had lighter hair and a mustache."

"So," Storm said, "What do you think happened that night?"

"I believe our killer attacked Elizabeth Stride, but was interrupted and had time only to cut her throat. He ran from the site, down Commercial Street and Aldgate, then saw Catherine Eddowes." Swanson looked over at Rowena who'd sat silent through most of the discussion.

"Fate wasn't with the woman this night. She'd been found earlier in the evening drunk and in a stupor. The PC took her to the station and she was put in a cell until she sobered. Approximately forty-five minutes before she was found murdered, she was released to go home. An officer last saw her walking toward Houndsditch."

"Oh, poor Catherine. If only she'd been kept a while longer, released a little later." Rowena's sad words were barely whispered, but both men sat quiet looking at her.

"Yes. Well," Swanson continued, "the rest you know. Eddowes was killed and horribly mutilated. He seems to have made quick work of the job as at least one witness believes he saw her talking to a gentleman only a few minutes before she was found. Of course I don't put a great lot of faith in such statements. It would have taken more than a few minutes to do what was done too her."

"I can't understand why Catherine would have let someone covered in blood come so close to her. I know it was dark but the murderer's clothing would have been wet and smelled of blood from Liz Stride."

"It's a question I'd like answered

myself, my lady." Swanson shook his head. "And this gentleman the witness saw was not so marked. He was seen standing in a light talking to the woman."

"Then the witness must have seen a different man and woman," de Grey stated. "We all know that cutting the throat of a living being creates a great deal of blood to be let."

"Or perhaps," Rowena said thoughtfully, "what the witness saw was as an accomplice. Perhaps the *gentleman* stopped and offered her an enticement. If she was on her way home so late she would know John Kelly, the man she lived with, would be outraged. Perhaps she thought money would appease him. I know Catherine didn't regularly practice prostitution, but if she was offered enough..."

"You're suggesting there are two killers?" Swanson asked incredulously. "You're the one who insisted the killer is always the same person."

"No, not two killers, one who acts and one who observes."

"A possibility," de Grey commented his face thoughtful. "But wouldn't such a combination cause more difficulty trying to avoid capture?"

"I don't think so. One gentleman watches then goes off in another direction from the killer. Maybe he even has a coach and they arrange to meet at some point. Then the killer is driven away. The observer could divert the constables as they patrol, tipping a hat, a nice good night, a few words to cause delay. It would distract them long enough for his fiendish friend to pass them by in another street or alley on the way to the meeting place. Then again, these are just ramblings."

"But possibilities. The constables have regular times they are meant to pass through the areas they patrol. If I was the killer, I'd certainly know the schedule and have my accomplice work to slow their steps," Swanson said.

"And a moment or two's delay wouldn't be something the PC would have to account for in their patrol records. They'd think it was irrelevant." de Grey agreed. "You may have struck on something Rowena."

"Perhaps." She smiled ruefully. "But it gets us no closer to the identity of the killer or his accomplice, if he has one."

Storm turned toward Swanson. "So what of this piece of apron and the writing on the wall I've heard about?"

"That was surely mucked up by the City police. The sergeant had the words washed from the wall before the police photographer arrived to take pictures. He was afraid the crowd gathering would begin to attack the Jews, who are the majority of residents in the area. As for the apron, it matched the one the woman wore. Perhaps it was cut off to carry the souvenirs, for lack of a better word, taken from her body. Perhaps he had another container to hold them and didn't want to be too close to her when he stopped to put them into it."

As the hour was nearing dinnertime, Rowena went to ask the cook to prepare something simple for her guests. When it was ready they retired to the dining room and by unspoken agreement talked of matters unrelated to murder. Afterward they again retired to the library, where de Grey acted as host pouring the whiskey and sherry.

He's too comfortable here. And I find it too comfortable to have him here. If only it weren't necessary to see him and include him in these discussions.

"I'm trying not to feel guilty all these women were patients." Rowena cast a glance at each of the men. "Logically I

302

know I'm not responsible, but why these women? There were special to me. They all came to see me at one time or another. They all lived in the poorest conditions and I believe most along the same street, but what made him select them?

"Perhaps you're the link, Row," Storm spoke softly.

She cut her eyes toward him, silently warning him again against using the nickname he had given her.

Ignoring her, he continued. "Maybe someone hates you, or thinks you've done something unforgivable, but even as I say the words, I can't believe such a thing."

"It may not be so direct," Swanson said. "We're not dealing with someone who reasons like we do. Lady Radcliffe doesn't have to be the object of attention. There could be a connection to the building, or the fact someone saw each of them on the street at a particular time of the day."

Rowena felt tears gathering in her eyes but blinked them back. "I'm taking this too personally."

Swanson looked at the papers he'd brought with him. "But will knowing your theories and all this speculation help us find the killer?"

"Possibly, there are no certainties, however it may help you to determine who among your suspects is not a candidate."

Storm asked, "Is there anything about this man we know as fact?"

"Very little. My lady, can you give me a clearer understanding of the type of person we're looking for, in your opinion?"

Rowena gathered her thoughts. "As you know Doctor Bond and I have been corresponding with each other on this matter. He believes this is a solitary man, nineteen to fifty-five years of age who has trouble holding a job. The man has a hatred of all women and is suffering from a sexual aberration, as well as being mentally unstable. There are points I don't agree with. I am not sure this is a solitary man. I believe a partnership is quite possible. But we both agree that there is only one killer, and though he doesn't have any special knowledge of anatomy as a doctor or butcher would, he certainly has general knowledge as would someone who slaughters animals have."

"So, where else do you think Doctor Bond is incorrect?" Swanson looked down at the notes he had taken of what had been said.

"I think it's possible this person appears normal to those around him. If he were mentally unstable, in the manner Thomas believes, he would stand out and people would notice. These women, though most were prostitutes, would never allow someone of that type so close, unless of course the theory of an accomplice drawing them in is correct."

"You may be right," Swanson said encouraging her to continue.

"I don't believe he has a hatred of all women. If this were so I believe we would have more attacks, some successful, some unsuccessful. Tales of these would have surfaced during the interviews. The women on the streets may not trust the police, but they're frightened and would mention something of this nature."

"Rowena," Garret said, "I don't believe you quite understand the relationships these women have with men. Though some men may return to the same, umm, unfortunate woman again and again, their usual customers are strangers. It is therefore much easier to approach them and cause them harm."

"Since when have you stumbled on your words?" She smiled. "I thought we agreed we can speak our minds to each other."

"Yes, but I didn't wish to upset or startle Swanson, here." Garret laughed. "Forgive me. I'll be forthright from this point."

Rowena smiled. "If you'll permit me I'd like to continue on these thoughts. There are other groups of women such as the housewives of the vigilance members or certainly their servants who might have been accosted but the killer is intent, I believe, on only these specific women."

"The citizens would be demanding assistance immediately if anyone had been threatened," Swanson agreed.

"I find it strange they all know each other so well. There are many poor women living on those dark streets, but I know for a fact each of the women who have been killed were close friends. I can't help but wonder if this is one of the reasons they have been chosen by this fiend."

De Grey nodded. "What about the escalation of violence?"

"He's becoming angrier. Yes, he's escalating the violence of each attack for some reason we haven't been able to determine. I believe these women have been selected as the specific recipients of his wrath."

Swanson asked, "Is there any other area of disagreement with Doctor Bonds' assessment?"

"I think in this case you have to set aside what might be considered obvious. It is generally believed, by those of us trying to draw such conclusions, this type of attack may have some sexual meaning. Because the killer is directly stabbing or mutilating the sexual area of the body. However, I studied every one of these bodies, here and those as far away as Germany. I think in this case this hypothesis may not be correct."

"Why?

Glancing again at de Grey who sat listening without comment, she answered. "I don't think those wounds were a result of the fury of the attack. It is much harder to tell for sure on Eddowes body, but the other victims who were mutilated bore stab wounds that were deeper and more tearing across their chests. The wounds we are speaking of where the organs were removed are more deliberate and controlled."

Swanson appeared ready to disagree.

"I know you may think I'm incorrect, but you saw the fury of the attacks. You saw the damage done by the knife as it was driven angrily into the flesh. The wounds in the pubic area did not display this...rage."

"So what do you suspect this means?"

"I honestly don't know. There is something wrong with everything I've seen and everything I've heard, if you compare these killings with similar ones. I do think the last killing, Catherine's, was highly personal. None of the others had their faces mutilated in such a manner."

"So you believe the killer had some grudge against this victim?" Swanson considered the idea.

"Against them all, but I can't imagine what it would be. Another thing disturbs me. The men I've studied kill, mutilate, dismember their victims, but never have I heard of one who escalated quite so quickly and with such fury.

Thomas Bond believes each killing makes it easier for the killer to act out some new fantasy on the next victim and increase his destructiveness. Not here. The killings are inconsistent. The woman in Oxford had her abdomen slashed open, but Mary Tabram did not and there appeared there was sufficient opportunity.

Of the eight killings I believe I can attribute to him, only three have been so cruelly destroyed. This is not the escalation of a desire to do more harm. "

"There was a break in the increased violence," Swanson said, chewing on his pipe.

"Exactly. Perhaps the earlier victims were…practice. The killings here in London feel as though some pressure has been building and we are nearing some climax. It makes me wonder if the killer targeted these specific women, and the list is growing shorter as the fury increases. It seems to me there's something very personal here and if you discover it, you will discover who the murderer is."

De Grey looked at her for several moments "What is it you are not saying Rowena? I can see you are holding something back."

"You know me too well. It is a foolish idea that flitted through my mind, but I would rather think on it a bit before saying more."

You'd think me mad if I told you. I am beginning to believe these women actually did something that triggered the killer to decide they must die.

———

CHAPTER TWENTY-FIVE

Members of the Vigilance Committee delivered half a kidney and created quite a stir. It was presumably the one taken from Catherine Eddowes. Rumor said George Lusk had been so stricken by its receipt he'd taken his family away from the city. Rowena sat in the office of Chief Inspector Swanson, studying the newest note.

From hell
Mr Lusk
Sir

I send you half the Kidne I took from one woman prasarved it for you. tother piece I fried and ate it was very nice. I may send you the bloody knif that took it out if you only wate a whil longer

*Signed Catch me when
You can
Mishter Lusk.*

"I think the writer is telling Lusk he could become a victim. The rest of the letter appears to be written for the shock value." Rowena handed the paper back to Donald across the desk.

"I seriously doubt Lusk's in any danger. The person writing this is probably just annoyed at all of the publicity Lusk's been getting. If it is the killer, he'd want all the attention on him, not some committee." Swanson held the now-familiar pipe in his hand, ready to clamp it between his teeth.

Rowena smiled. "I notice you rarely smoke outside your office. Your pipe is a method of relieving some of the tension you feel when you're here?"

He glanced at the hand holding it. "Yes, I suppose. I asked de Grey to join us, but he had other business to attend to.

311

You don't like having him included, do you?"

"You've noticed? There's a bit of tension when we have to be together and it makes me uncomfortable. However, we are working hard to set our differences aside. I'm sorry you took note." *Sorry, but relieved my true feelings are not showing. I can't let Storm or anyone else know how much I regret we cannot return to the past.*

"No matter. I, too, suffer from tension. There is much to attend to and the demands from my superiors make it...difficult." Swanson lifted his shoulders in a shrug then bit down on the stem of his pipe.

"I understand the Chief Commissioner, Sir Warren, is being forced to submit his resignation."

Taking the pipe from his lips, Swanson nodded. "Too much has been in print. First the letter about a month ago from someone claiming to be the killer. The experts are sure it wasn't in the same hand as the others, but who knows if the others came from our killer. Then Warren ups and writes an article for the *Murray's Magazine*. Stupid. Can't blame the Home Office for being angry. It was so full of...rubbish."

Rowena worried her lip, thinking of all the stories that had appeared in the newspapers and magazines. "Everyone's on edge. I'd suppose people could easily lose their sense of perspective. Even the poor of Whitechapel are different these days. I'm just now beginning to see the women come back to the surgery for my help. I had wondered if they thought I was involved in some way. They stopped coming to the clinic about the same time you and Storm suggested I or my location may be a key."

She studied Swanson's face before continuing. "Don't worry, I'm not feeling guilty any more. It seems they were just changing their routines, worried they'd become victims. It appears they did not see a connection to my office."

"De Grey still has his men posted near you."

"I know. I see them every day. Occasionally one will falsify a complaint to have a reason to come in and assure himself I'm safe. It's almost funny. The women become quite excited for they find these men handsome and hope to entice them to accompany them when they leave. The men do a great job of blending in, appearing to be common laborers looking

313

for work, rather than the homeless rascals I thought they'd be."

"De Grey has a fine lot of men at his disposal. I'm sure you haven't met them all, nor have I. He tells me they're friends, gathered over time in the taverns and coffee houses, but I suspect they're much more than that. They have an admirable skill being able to blend into their surroundings and they appear to know what they are doing."

"I'm sure they're who he claims. He's spent years ignoring his duties, taking up with ruffians. I admit however, he hasn't become as coarse as I would have believed and has shown a great deal of responsibility in assisting you in this matter."

Swanson raised one brow in surprise. "You really believe that of him? I find him, well let's say, extremely competent in this operation. However, one never truly understands the nature of another. It's another reason it's often difficult to find a killer. So often you hear their friends and neighbors declare they are incapable of such acts."

Something pulled at her. Something she'd heard or seen? Try as she might she couldn't capture it. "No, one

314

never knows the true heart of another," she agreed. "I'm sure when this killer is found we'll stare upon his face in disbelief."

———

CHAPTER TWENTY-SIX

Storm was expected within the hour, but Rowena didn't want to wait to start looking at the reports the coroner had provided. The inquest of Catherine Eddowes had taken little time to return the same conclusion as they had reached for the other women who had been slain by this monster. A verdict of *willful murder against some person or persons unknown* was announced.

Removing the paperwork from the desk drawer, she saw a slip of paper she had written on a few days earlier as she had reviewed the documents relating to the other victims. The note contained only a single question.

Why did Annie go to the casual ward for treatment?

She slipped the page in with the paperwork she would take to the surgery the following day.

Reluctant to face all the gruesome details, she began to read the witness statements confirming Catherine's identity. She grieved for the people who had loved the woman and would forever be tortured by their last look as they had confirmed she was theirs. Skipping over the police officer's testimony as well as the London City Surgeon Frederick Browns', she shuffled the papers, coming to a list of Kate's personal possessions and treasures. Scanning past the description of the bloodied garments, Rowena burst into tears.

Garret opened the door, catching a glimpse of desolation on Rowena's face as she burst into heart-wrenching sobs. When he reached her, she stared unseeing at the papers clutched in her hand. Carefully, he removed them and set them on the desk, then lifted her out of her chair and carried her to the settee where he held her in his lap.

"Row, it's alright," he crooned softly, shaken when she didn't protest. Instead, she buried her face against his neck.

"Little one, you've seen too much." He rocked her gently as he ran his hand soothingly down her back until the storm began to pass. "It's too much to ask of yourself, seeing these women..."

She pushed away from him, shaking her head, the tears still glistening in her eyes.

God, she's beautiful.

"You don't have to continue..."

"It's not that...I was reading..." Her voice hitched. Taking a deep breath, she tried again. It's not that..."

He searched her face, waiting. Even now, with tear-stained cheeks and reddened nose, he wanted to pull her back to him, kiss her lips, make the hurt disappear.

"I was reading the list...of Catherine's belongings." Her voice cracked. "The soap."

"Soap? I don't understand..."

"Every time she came for treatment," her lips quivered, "she'd tell me someone...someone had taken the soap I gave her."

He knew he looked confused.

"On the list. She had all of it. Every piece, when she died." Tears welled up, but this time she blinked rapidly to dispel them.

"Oh, Row, I'm so sorry. It just makes the loss so personal for you. Perhaps you need to step away-"

"No. No. No. I'll not turn my back on her or the others. I know what I'm doing will help find their slayer." She pushed herself off his lap. Staring down at him, anger boiled up to replace the pain. "If you can't believe in me and give me your support, leave."

He started to snap back at her, then realized anger was far better than the grief which had threatened to overcome her. "I think you're just wasting your time and mine."

The anger in her eyes flared brighter.

"However, I have no choice but to let you do as you please. You've reminded me of this fact often enough these last months, as has Albany."

He watched her simmer, then turn striding to the bell to call Margaret. Silent until she made her request, she returned briskly, glaring at him as she took her seat at the desk. Only slightly more subdued, she handed him a set of documents.

"Let's begin with these."

———

They sat silently reading, making notes that seemed pertinent. Margaret stepped into the room. "My lady, there's a man at the door, says he's the police photographer, brought you some photos he made copies of for you."

"Tell him to come in."

"What do you think of this new trend, photographing the victims?" Storm set the report he was reading on the chair beside him.

"It's certainly been a help to identifying those who have died without proper identification on them. I think it might also be beneficial to record the scenes of murders. Memory is not one hundred percent, even with the men who continuously investigate the crimes. Small pieces of information can be lost when they don't have the opportunity to write a complete report immediately after they leave a scene."

"Exactly, my lady." The young man took off his hat as he walked toward them. "I'm Thomas Black. DI Abberline is a friend and thought you might want to have a look at these. The ones of Eddowes are pretty bad though, except the last. Waited for rigor, stood her up to the wall to take that one." He grinned as he handed the package to de Grey.

Rowena felt her stomach flip as she smiled queasily. "Thank you. This is Lord de Grey." She couldn't say more as she looked at Storm, hoping he would say something about the man's callous attitude. It wasn't the pictures, but the apparent enjoyment the man took in his position.

"Yes, thank you." Garret gave her a what-do-you-want-me-to-say smile and set the package aside before he stood and walked to the sideboard. "Would you care for a drink?"

"No sir...my lord, I've got to be back to home case I be needed again."

"Then, thanks again, Mr. Black. We appreciate you having made the delivery in person."

"Had to, my lord, can't let this lot get out ta' others." Tipping his hat before setting it back on his head, he smiled again and excused himself.

"Well, certainly nice to see someone who appears to enjoy his work so much," Storm drawled.

Rowena laughed. "I'm not quite

sure what to make of him. He doesn't seem too affected by what he's seen. Poor Kate, being stood up against a wall, I presume, after all the other indignity she's had to suffer, it was little enough."

"I think we can save these for later." He returned to his chair, and moved the package off the desk, to the seat beside him. "These reports are enough for one day."

"So, what have you got?"

Glancing through his notes, he sat back and looked up toward the ceiling. "Not much. All of the doctors agree that the cuts to the throat were from left to right. That appears to be about as far as the agreement goes."

"I think it gives us a vital piece of information. The killer uses his left hand."

"What makes you say such a thing? Wouldn't it depend on how the victims were attacked?"

"I believe the killer was in *front* of them or just to the side as he drew the knife across their throats. It would be very awkward for a right-handed person to make the cut in the direction of the wounds."

"Why in front? Wouldn't it make more sense the killer came at them from behind?"

"I think most of the women were lying on the ground when they were killed. It would be impossible to come up from behind if this was the case."

"I remember you saying you thought the Chapman woman may have been bent forward against the wall. If I understood correctly, it was because of the blood splashed on the wall, a foot or so above the ground. If the murderer was left handed the cut on her throat would have been from right to left."

"True, unless they held the knife in their right hand on that occasion. It would explain why this cut was so jagged. In each of the other cases where the killer rendered them silent, the cut was much cleaner."

"But why would this fiend change how he assaulted them?"

"That's a question I've pondered, and the only reason I can think of is Kate knew her killer and wouldn't have let him so close if she got a good look at him."

Storm sat silently, absorbing what Rowena had proposed. The more he thought about it, it seemed as solid a theory as any he'd heard to date. "Okay, so what does this offer us?"

"If I'm correct we can eliminate

Lee Leslie

anyone who is right handed from the suspects."

"So, do you think the killer is a physician?" Garrett teased.

"Actually I don't," she responded, knowing he was making fun of her, yet taking a serious tone. "I know this is something these other doctors have said often enough, especially since the kidney was removed. However as I told you before, I believe they are pompous old dragons."

Storm coughed out a strangled laugh. "Now, tell me why you should think such a thing? I have to admit, my lady, you have set my sensibilities on edge of late."

She sat silent, glaring at him for the briefest moment.

"I know we agreed to speak freely in front of each other, but I thought I knew you better. A 'damnation' here, a 'bloody hell' there, I find it quite refreshing. So why are they...dragons?"

"Even the investigators who admit someone other than a doctor could know where organs are within the body believe only a man could perform these cruelties. Although I might agree a man is responsible for these atrocities, doctors, butchers, and hunters are not the only ones

324

who know how the inner body in constructed. It is as though they cannot get their minds out of the city."

"I'm not sure I understand." Storm stood and helped himself to a drink.

"Every farmer, farm hand, farmer's wife and their children come in contact with the slaughter of animals. And on many farms, the wife and daughters perform some or all of the cleaning of the animals to prepare them for drying or cooking."

"I admit I wouldn't think of such a thing myself."

"I feel the men, especially the doctors, who treat me as though I'm unfit to be a woman because I wish to be part of their world, have blinders on that can cause the investigators serious problems."

"So, and I ask hesitantly, you are saying the killer could be a woman?" Storm crossed back to his chair and dropped into it, setting the glass on the edge of the desk.

"NO. I am saying there are millions of people in this city who would know enough to...just suppose the killer wanted the kidney because they had already thought of sending it to George Lusk, with the taunting little note. Anyone who cooks steak and kidney pie is going to have some idea of what the organ looks like."

"Go on."

"If I know what I'm looking for, and there is a limited amount of area to search for it, I am very likely going to look and poke about until I find it."

"Do you think there was time for this poking?"

"As we discussed, if the killer knew the routes and times the PC's adhere to, it is more than likely they were sure they had the time. If you add a possible accomplice, who takes a minute or two to distract the constable, you are absolutely sure to have the time."

"What if someone not a constable came across the murder?"

"I believe in such a case you would have found a witness or two unable to testify, as they would have joined our victims."

———

"Doctor Parker, I realize it's been a while, but I'm hoping you will remember treating a patient of mine." Rowena smiled at the man sitting across from her. He leaned forward, as if eager to hear every word.

"Dr. Radcliffe, I don't remember

anyone around here. We're really quite busy, as you can see by those outside the door waiting to be seen. Too many people. Often we don't get to treat everyone who's waiting."

"The city's grown too fast these last few years. I've read recently the population is well over three million people. I can't even imagine such a number.

"Yes, and as fast as it grows, the population of the poor grows faster. I can't imagine why so many come here and don't leave when they find there's little for them."

"Perhaps they have nowhere else to go," Rowena said. "Even with all those you see, I think perhaps you may remember this one lady. She came to see you not long before she died. Her name was Annie Chapman."

Benjamin pushed back, his eyes wide. "Of course. I believe I treated her just the day before the sad event. She was a...an interesting woman. She was in great pain, yet smiled and even joked a bit as I tried to help her."

"Yes she had a way about her, looking at even dark moments with a hopeful attitude. I wondered if you could tell me when she was here. I was saddened to hear she had gone to another for help."

"Oh, it was rather late, so I would guess you had closed your office for the day. She was feeling very poorly. I gave her a bit of laudanum and some vitamins, though I didn't tell her that is all they were. Her cousin brought her in."

"Cousin? I wasn't aware she had one in the area."

"A rather odd duck. Colorless, if you know what I mean."

"I believe I do. Is there anything else you can tell me about the cousin? I would be interested in finding her and offering my condolences."

"No. She really was not memorable. I'm sorry I can't tell you more."

Rowena rose from her chair, collecting her pocketbook and medical bag. "Well I won't bother you further, and I appreciate your taking the time to talk."

Rowena considered what Doctor Parker had told her. It made perfect sense Annie would have called at the ward if she had become suddenly ill after the surgery was closed and she had gone home for the night. Yet the other bit of information nagged at her. Who was this cousin, and why hadn't this person stepped forward or been mentioned during the investigation?

CHAPTER TWENTY-SEVEN

Garret took the offered seat as he sat across the desk from Albany.

"So have you found out anything? Are the police having any luck in finding this madman?"

"No, Your Grace, there's nothing to report. Almost everything known you can read in the papers. Chief Inspector Swanson is a dedicated man. He's doing all he can to track the killer and is as frustrated as we are."

"The Queen is not happy over this matter. She's outraged by the rumors about her family being involved. Do Lady

Radcliffe or Swanson suspect you are working for the Royals?"

"No, they believe what I've told them. I've acquaintances of low regard, loyal to my service that are willing to offer their assistance."

"I imagine there is fire between you and the lady. I believe at one time you thought yourself in love with her."

"Your spies are very efficient and you know me too well." Storm clenched his jaw before continuing. "I *am* in love with her. When she left for America then decided to attend medical school, it hurt. I had hoped she would wait for me. However, I couldn't follow, as you well know. Since then I've recovered sufficiently to act my part in this play. Even if I should try to change things she's not willing to give me another chance."

"I am sorry, de Grey, your service has caused you pain of a kind I can't help you to overcome. I watched the two of you as you grew up. You and Rowena were good together, but your calling was destined. I can't change the past for you."

"I understand the position you're in, my lord," de Grey admitted sitting back into the chair and crossing his legs in an attempt to give the appearance of surrender.

Albany rose and walked to the fireplace, placing his hand on the mantle and watching Storm from the corner of his eye. "You never told her you were working for me? The situation that caused your problems was not of your making?"

"I keep the oath I took to your service. I admit I believed she'd understand. Somehow know I wasn't the man she saw gambling, drinking...going over this is fruitless and has no bearing on my current duties."

"You're politely saying it's none of my business." Albany smiled, satisfied Garret was telling the truth. "However, I do enjoy the matters of the heart. All right, what of Lord Sheffield? Have you been able to determine what he's doing, how he might be involved in this?"

"If he is, he's extremely cautious. My men haven't been successful uncovering any evidence against him or that woman he keeps near. The pair of them went to one of his country estates a few weeks ago. I expect he'll be back soon."

"His absence could lend credence to your theories. He's been away and nothing more has occurred."

331

"Or it doesn't mean anything. I had one of my men go into the house, but he wasn't able to make a full sweep. He did search through Sheffield's correspondence and there was nothing, not even a word on a blotter, to confirm our suspicions."

"So your men are following him when he's here in town?"

"We tried, but he's too aware of what's happening around him. I thought it best to end the assignment. The men who did follow the few times he went out at night, were led on a merry chase about the town with no apparent purpose other than to make it obvious he was aware of their presence."

"Perhaps he's not involved. You've never liked him and I can't say you harbor no prejudice in that quarter. I find it difficult to believe one of his stature is going about killing whores."

"You may be right, but I find his interests exceedingly disgusting. He's a morbid man who asks too many questions about the horrors and gruesome details and has worked too hard, though unsuccessfully, to insinuate himself into the investigation."

"So we have nothing to show for all these efforts."

De Grey rose to leave. "We won't give up, your grace. We can't. I know we're on the right path. Proving it is a different matter."

"We'll talk again soon," he called out as Storm reached the door. "De Grey, she's a beautiful woman, not only of body, but also of heart. I think you should work harder to win her back."

———

Rowena spent the afternoon working on matters unrelated to the killings. Still disturbed by the sensation she'd overlooked something, she hoped by turning her attention to the more mundane tasks of running a household, whatever it was would surface of its own accord.

Marchioness Ulster called at tea, filled with excitement about the charitable efforts she'd become embroiled in. She and her friends had been hard at work to establish a school to train young women finding themselves in unfortunate circumstances to serve in the households of those who could provide them hope for the future. Their first graduates, as she called them, had been well placed, but only after she and her peers had been satisfied their new employers would not hold their pasts against them.

"Your recommendations have been very useful, Rowena. I'm proud of the work we've done and am hoping to find someone to help us get more of these poor girls out of the workhouses and factories. Several of us actually toured one of those horrible places. We caused quite a disturbance, showing up unannounced and demanding to be let in. It was wonderful."

"Even more wonderful is your commitment. There're so many who have the means to assist and don't care to do so."

Setting down her cup, the Marchioness rose. "Well, I must be going. My dear husband will want me to attend the dinner he's giving tonight. He's been so excited about the work I'm doing, he's decided to try to do something for the young men in those places. It's not a revolution, but perhaps we can win more over to our cause."

"That's admirable, I hope him great success." Rowena walked with the Marchioness to the door, thanking her for her enthusiasm. For the first time in days, her heart felt lighter. She'd seen the worst horrors men could do, but she was also a part of the goodness that could come from the hearts of others.

"Oh, my dear, I so forget with all the excitement over our ladies, did you hear the scandal? Those boys Sheffield took aboard this year were found abusing some of the poor women in those horrible streets of Whitechapel. Lady Farendale, who is a close friend, said the constables dragged them home when they were discovered and wouldn't leave until the parents were apprised of the situation. I understand they have been shipped off to their country estates as punishment."

Stunned, Rowena said nothing, just smiled half-heartedly as the woman exited the house. She watched her carriage pull away from the curb, replaying the last bit of conversation in her head before returning to her study and pulling the reports from her surgery and from the police departments to go over them. The boys. Something about the boys tugged at her mind as she read through the paperwork.

———

Sheffield had gone out to dinner the moment they arrived back in town. He was tired of the whiney little bitch and needed some time to himself. Returning home late, he'd gone directly to his office only to find someone had been through his correspondence.

He started up the stairs to her room, but stopped. It was late, he was tired, and this could wait until morning. If it had been her, she would pay for her sin in ways she'd never dreamed of and would find most unpleasant. The thought made him smile.

———

Morgana cringed as Sheffield walked into the library.

"What have you been up to? You look guilty. Are you the one who's gone through my desk?"

"No."

"Ah, Morgana, don't lie to me. I know everything you've done. Everything you do. Everything you think."

"Truly, I'd never do such a thing." She began to shake as he stared at her. "I only come in to deliver the paper. I always place it on your desk as you require."

"Damnation, then who's been here and searched my things? Only you would have the audacity. The others are sniveling cowards and would never touch anything."

"Is something missing?"

"No, and that disturbs me more. Whoever it was is looking for information, not planning on stealing from me." He paused and looked over at her, enjoying the fear he saw in her eyes. "Has anyone been in your rooms my dear?"

"They can't have. I keep it well locked when I'm about the house."

He stared. "And when you're not? Like these weeks we've been gone?"

"Your treasures are well hidden. I only display them when you're expected." She twisted her hands as she spoke, trembling harder.

An evil smile curved his lips. "Yes, the little treasures I've entrusted to you. I think you should put them out this evening. I may pay a visit. We need to prepare for what is to come and I think I'll enjoy a bit of your company. You have been very irritating of late and you need to be punished."

Morgana's eyes glowed. "Yes, master Sheffield. I'll prepare everything."

—

Lee Leslie

CHAPTER TWENTY-EIGHT

The carriage rolled to a stop outside the surgery. Just as she collected her things and prepared to exit, a lad ran by shouting a murder had been committed only a short distance away. Rowena instructed Fagan to deliver her to the address as quickly as he could.

Dorset Street was narrow and dark. The buildings seemed to groan with the weight of the sorrow their walls had seen. Broken windows, doors falling from their frames added to the desolation of the area. How could people live in such hopeless surroundings? The ones who did had surely lost their ability to dream of better days. This street was said to be one of the most violent in all of London. If this murder had been done by their killer, nothing short of tearing it all down would remove the stigma of such a label.

She feared what she was going to see. Knowing how quickly the fury of the killer had escalated, she tried to prepare herself for a nightmare. The coach slowed as they moved though the street where a crowd was already beginning to grow. Fagan threatened to run over someone more than once when they didn't wish to get out of his way.

Only two constables stood outside the building.

"My lady, how did you arrive so quickly?"

"I heard the shouts of a lad and came immediately. Where is your help? You won't be able to keep those people away for long."

"We followed the man who found the body back here from the station, but others will be here soon."

Just as he finished speaking, she saw de Grey striding down from the far end of the street toward her with one of the Detective Inspectors. Behind them a number of PC's were pushing back the crowd gathered at that end, and several of the force were moving their way to help with crowd control at her end of the lane where the onlookers where already growing restless.

"May I look?"

"It's a sight I don't believe I'll ever forget. You have to look inside through the side window, the door to the room is locked."

She stepped over to where he directed and moved the coat that hung over the window aside. As her eyes adjusted, she finally saw the most recent horror. The small room held hardly more than the bed and a chair where a dress was flung over the back. What remained of the woman, who would later be identified as Mary Kelly, lay on the narrow bed. A small table beside it held a bloody mass of flesh.

The body was tilted forward toward the window. Blood was splattered on the walls. It appeared her breasts had been removed, meat from the thigh had clearly been cut off and the bone was exposed on the one leg bent at the knee. The killer had slashed at the face time and again until you couldn't recognize any of the woman's features.

She felt sick. She clutched at her stomach as it roiled with the shock and horror at the fury it had taken to do such complete destruction. Feeling light-headed she stepped back, taking a deep breath and closing her eyes in a fruitless effort to block out the gruesome scene. It would have been impossible to imagine what one human could do to another had she not seen it for herself.

She was almost sure the murder had occurred just this morning, perhaps not more than an hour ago, as the dark stains still had the wet glisten of fresh blood. She looked over at the young constable who still looked a bit green in the face. "Have you learned anything from the neighbors yet? Did they hear anything?"

"It's already confusing a bit. The neighbor across the street says she saw the woman, Mary Jane Kelly, out this morning, about eight, but another says it wasn't her. A third said they saw a woman leave her room about fifteen minutes before the body was found. That's just a bit ago."

"Would you mind if I talked to her?"

"She's over there talking to Dew."

Glad she'd arrived before the crowd had begun to swell, she stepped to the side of the constable pointed out as Dew and listened while she formulated her own questions.

"I saw her standing at the end of the street. She looked like she was waitin' for someone. A man was in the distance but I couldn't make out 'is face. I thought maybe he was gonna' take 'er to 'er cousin she'd been talkin' about."

"Her cousin? I thought you said she didn't have any family in the area," the PC said, looking down at the notes in his hand.

"I don't know the woman was really her cousin, 'cause when Flat Bitsy called 'er that Mary'd laugh right out loud real hard, kind'a like is was a nasty joke. I never seen the woman close-up, but once I saw her goin' in. She was bigger than Mary, brownish hair pulled back from her face, looked like it would hurt to be bound up so tight. Mary said she 'ad money but ya' couldn't tell by the way she dressed."

The description of the woman's hair. A bloody dress tossed over a chair in the room she had just viewed. The pattern in the material faded. Almost unrecognizable. Rowena's mind whirled as memories flooded through her. She began to put together the words of the witness with what she suspected. What she knew.

The image of Mary and her friends backed into a corner in the surgery as Rowena's assistant battered them with words of gospel. The look on their faces. A combination of fear and contempt.

Ridiculous. Why would a nurse, someone who was dedicated to helping others, harm the woman? Was it even feasible? Rowena had argued that the doctors and investigators overlooked the abilities of a woman to commit such a crime, but she had never believed it could really happen. Had she?

She could feel the blood drain from her face as she thought of her childhood friend. A man who liked those around him to think he was a bad boy, but in reality was weak and could easily be taken advantage of. Did he know? *No. Of course not.* He wanted to be in the center of things, that was how he had always been, but the smallest drop of blood from a paper cut made him sick at his stomach. There was no way he could be a party to something like this.

She had to tell him. Warn him.

Rowena rushed to her carriage, ordering Fagan to take her to the address where she knew she would find the killer. Her heart beat like thunder in her chest, as

Fagan fought to make way for the carriage through the crowd. She hoped she was wrong but it had been right there in the room for anyone to see. She knew the question that had nagged at her of late had been answered.

CHAPTER TWENTY-NINE

The door to the house stood open. Blood smeared the floor and staircase. Silently she followed the telling trail. Entering the room where the path ended she saw Bradley Sheffield's hand sliding up the blood-encrusted bodice of the dress Morgana wore, coming to rest as it covered her breast. Mary Kelly's shawl was thrown across the end of the bed.

"Rowena. We weren't expecting you." Sheffield looked out the door to the staircase. "Naughty girl. Aren't you always scolding me for dropping in unannounced?"

"I came to warn you—"

Cruel laughter rang though the room.

"Now, now Morgana. It isn't polite to laugh at our guest." He took a step away from the nurse, toward Rowena. "I'm surprised you came alone Row. I would have thought you would bring de Grey. Aren't you afraid to be here alone?"

"I didn't think you knew. I was sure she had tricked you but that's not right, is it? Have you known from the beginning? Did you encourage her to kill? I don't understand what's happened to you Bradley. What did she do to make you change?" But it was suddenly clear. She was finally seeing Bradley as he really was. He had tried to warn her months ago when they had met at the inn outside London. He had been trying to make her see he had changed. He had fallen into the abyss. It wasn't an act any more.

"I can see you remember now. I told you. Expect the worst. You've always been so sensitive to others. Knew they were cruel and evil. Why couldn't you see me as I really am? However, it has been fun to watch you search for the answers when it was all right there in front of you."

Morgana stepped back. Hatred and triumph glowed from her face as she straightened and laughed. "He's been my mentor, my *lady*. He told me what he wanted and I practiced hard to give him just that. You always thought you're so much better than me, but you're *nothing*. I am the hand of God. Bradley is the rod that saves me from my sins. Not that he can wield the knife, of course. If you know him you are aware he can't stand the site of fresh blood, but I've been working on him. Helping him to see it is purifying."

Rowena glanced about the room, feeling even sicker as she noted the shackles attached to the four posts of the narrow bed, more hanging from the ceiling, where dark maroon blotches were most assuredly not paint. A whip lay precisely curled at the foot of the narrow, Spartan bed. A case holding surgical implements sat on a small table by the window.

She must have used the knives to slay her victims.

Jars filled with clear liquid, alcohol or wine, sat on a shelf in front of the room's small window. The organs removed from the women floated in the sunlight.

Finally, she looked up. Her eyes searched first Sheffield's face, then the woman's who stood next to him. Rowena wanted to curl up like a baby, and shut out this horrifying discovery. She hoped the whole scene and the people in it were just part of a hideous nightmare and she would awaken at any moment. *Why didn't I tell someone what I suspected? Did I really believe Sheffield would protect me from this woman?*

Morgana lovingly ran her hands over the blade of one of the knives which sat atop the open case, stained with drying blood. "I see you've noticed my *toys*. I took these fine tools from my former employer's surgery. You know he passed away very conveniently. His family never questioned what happened to him. They were sure he had drifted off quietly in his sleep."

"Why? I don't understand." She felt her anger rise as Bradley stood beside the Ridley woman, smiling arrogantly. "How could you encourage her to do such things?" She shuddered as she looked into his dark, flat eyes and realized what little care he'd once had had disappeared.

"Row. Dear pathetic little fool. I've never lied to you. Not once. I made it clear I enjoy my entertainments. Surely you didn't believe having children trail after me across the continents was pleasurable. Nor are card games, hours of boring balls, the foolishness of people wrapped up in their daily, torturous lives. I craved excitement, deserved it. Taking risks, what a wonderful thrill. Wondering if we'd be found out. Seeing those fools who were hanged pay for *our* sins. All the while enjoying the joy of watching my sweet lady demonstrate her passion for God's work."

"You call this God's work? This slaughter? I'd wager Satan himself finds what you've done sickening. You must give yourself up, Bradley. Morgana. You can't believe what you've done is righteous. This last murder...only the horrors of war could equal the mutilation and the anger that drove you to do this-"

"Mary Jane got all she deserved," Morgana spat. "I only wish she'd lived through to the end of what I did to her."

"I don't understand. How could anyone deserve such a death?"

Sheffield looked over to the blood-soaked woman. "Lady Radcliffe won't carry this tale. Tell her why you slay the demons."

Sheffield's smile sent chills along Rowena's spine. Her heart tripped frantically as she watched him reach for a pistol that lay on the table by the surgical kit.

"*Mary Kelly*. My *loving* cousin and her good friend Kate. Mary recognized me when she saw me shopping. She and her vile friends laughed...LAUGHED at me. Taunted me for having been able to rise above them," she spat, her anger growing. "Dear, sweet Mary, threatened me. Thought she could make me pay to keep her quiet."

Morgana's smile turned Rowena's heart to ice.

"She demanded I come visit her where she and that Eddowes woman sat plotting how they'd tell the world I'd been one of them. They were immoral, sinning whores."

"So you killed five women to keep them from telling someone you'd been a prostitute?" Bile rose in Rowena's throat.

"It was more than that. I'd turned poor Mary out when she was just a child. She said I *owed* her for ruining her life. She demanded money again and again." Morgana sneered. "I made them think they had me. Even gave them a few shillings here and there. Then I started getting rid of their friends."

"Tell me-"

Morgana's cruel laugh echoed through the room, "I even got a bit of fun making myself up. *My* favorite was Annie. I was done up as a lad, so Bradley could introduce me to the ways of women. Oh, she was a bit of fun. My lord calling her into the yard, telling her she would be my first. She didn't recognize me, too far into her cups. As he instructed she lifted her skirts, bent forward to lean against the wall, ready to accept me. Surprised she was when I reached round and slit her throat. Bradley spewed his stomach into his hat. It was the first time he actually saw me take a knife to one of the whores."

Rowena struggled not to show the disgust she felt.

"I wanted to save Kate and Mary for last," Morgana said quietly, staring somewhere behind Rowena. Remembering? "Make them sweat a bit. Wonder who the killer was. See if they knew they were on the list. You know the rest."

What else had she done? "Were the letters to the papers...did you write them?

Morgana's eyes glowed. "No, sweet Bradley had that idea. He thought you caught on the night you were here at dinner and noticed the ink on the blotter. You can imagine the laugh we had over your lack of insight after that letter got delivered and no constables came to call."

How could I miss it? Why was I so blind? "The package to George Lusk?"

"That was another fine idea. Stupid man. Primping about for the papers as if he were important. He told the world he would find me and hadn't a clue who I was. I went to that first meeting where they ask for volunteers. Stood next to him as he talked about the description of the killer he'd gotten from a secret source. How he'd break the case open. I wish I'd had my tools while I listened to him puff up like one of those hot air balloons." Morgana crooned.

Rowena forced herself to remain calm. She thought she heard a sound in the hallway outside the door but was afraid to look. She prayed one of the servants, overhearing the conversation, was on their way to collect her driver Fagan and the police.

———

CHAPTER THIRTY

Rowena needed to keep them distracted. "Were you also responsible for Emma Smith?" She forced down the fear that threatened to overwhelm her, praying they couldn't hear it in her voice.

"I'm afraid her death was an unfortunate accident," Sheffield smirked. "A little reunion with my lads. It went a bit badly. They were only tormenting her, but she became over frightened."

His laughter raked over her.

"I was just standing against the building watching the fun as she ran from them. She almost impaled herself on the head of my favorite walking cane, the one with the silver handle. You know how I like to carry it in the horizontal, so I can poke at the beggars."

She'd seen Storm do the same.

"Unfortunately the boys, after reading of her demise, haven't been anxious to join me in those pursuits again. "

"Bradley," she said his name softly, "you taught those boys to torture those who did them no harm? What did you do to the girls?"

"Well, I really don't need to explain any of that to you, do I? They were...conveniences. Someone to toy with and keep the boredom at bay. Of course, I had to work on them a bit, threatened them that they'd end up like the women in those dull towns we visited. I took them out to see the last one, there in Oxford. After all, I had to make sure they didn't run straight to mum and da' when they returned home."

"God in heaven, you didn't-

"Well," Sheffield rolled his eyes. "I didn't tell them we did that, or let them watch. I just showed them what happened to dirty little whores."

"Oh, you don't know nearly as much as you think." Morgana's eyes narrowed as a sickening smile drew up her thin lips.

"I learned of Lord Sheffield's desire for special entertainment as we all traveled about. First I went off by myself in Germany. Later, when I told him how I wanted to please him, we selected the most desirable for him to occupy himself with before I struck."

Sheffield ran his hand down Morgana's back.

"I waited in the carriage until he charmed them to take a drive. You know what happened to them after they agreed."

"It was simple. I accompanied Morgana and caught them just like fish, pulling them in. All they had to do was see fancy clothes and they were more than willing to do anything I asked.

"Do we have to go into the details of every little gratification we've enjoyed lately? As pleasurable as it's been, I don't wish to dwell on the past."

"But my lord, I want her to know how much she's helped us. How in working at the surgery I was able to find where each of the whores lived. Put a good bit over on you, my lady. Helping that trash. I put a bit of arsenic in your precious salve and sent a few of your patients to hell."

"You poisoned woman who came to

355

me for help?" *I knew something was wrong but never put it together. How could I be so blind?*

"And you never suspected a thing. Not even when their friends cried sad tears for their sudden and unexpected loss. It took great control not to laugh in your face as you offered them your sympathy. Of course, my lord Sheffield wasn't aware of this until I left your service."

"Well, enough bragging for one day, my love. I'm afraid we're going to have to decide what to do with our lovely Rowena."

"It should be easy enough. We'll hold her here until late tonight. She'll be found tomorrow or the next day murdered by one of her ungrateful patients in her surgery."

Rowena could see the effect of Morgana's words. It was impossible not to notice the bulge in Sheffield's trousers as the woman called him master again and began to describe the method of death she was planning.

Her stomach roiled violently, while she fought for composure. Desperately she dared a glance toward the door. She was stunned as she glimpsed Storm pressed against the wall in the shadow outside the door. She'd never been so glad to see him. *If I live through this, I'll forgive him for everything, past, present, and future.*

He held a pistol in one hand and placed a finger to his lips with the other, warning her to remain silent.

Sheffield's voice drew her back. "Yes, yes you're quite right. But it is such a waste. Row has been a good friend to me." He glanced from Morgana to Rowena. "It can't be helped. I know. I'll go with you and watch."

"We must get rid of her driver and carriage. Guess your Fagan will have to die as well." Morgana laughed.

"Such a shame." Sheffield handed the firearm to Morgana, stroking her blood-covered breasts one last time, then walked toward Rowena, careful not to put himself between the two women.

"I'll miss you." He gently caressed Rowena's face and neck. She smelled the powerful scent of blood and death on his hands. "You're one of the few people in this world I haven't found boring."

He actually looked saddened at the thought. Then suddenly he smiled, leaning a bit closer to whisper in her ear. "Of course if you wish to live we can dispose of

Morgana and you can help me with my games."

"Never."

"Oh, well then, it can't be helped."

He leaned forward, as though to kiss her. As he took a half step forward she brought her hand up and slapped his face with all her strength.

A scream of rage issued from Morgana as she dropped the gun on the table and rushed forward, claws extended. Rowena could see her intent on tearing her eyes out with her bare hands. Grabbing for Sheffield's cane which was propped next to her against the bed, she was surprised when it came apart and a knife glistened in her hand.

Sheffield, eyes blazing murderously, was suddenly jerked back then sent sailing across the room, into the furious woman's path just as Rowena turned to defend herself. The knife sliced through him.

Unable to stop her forward movement Morgana collided with him. Together they fell into a blood-covered heap at Rowena's feet.

"Storm." Rowena's teeth chattered and she swayed, afraid she was going to faint. Shocked, she didn't notice how badly

Sheffield had been injured.

Storm grabbed her arm and gently settled her on the edge of the bed as the clatter of men could be heard at the base of the stairs. Keeping his gun pointed at the two people struggling to untangle themselves, he backed toward the door as footsteps pounded up the stairway. He watched the late arrivals from the police rush in, mouths open as they took in the scene.

———

"How did you know?" Rowena drew the coat Storm had wrapped around her tighter. Detectives Abberline and Andrews had removed the couple to separate rooms downstairs, while Storm led her from the attic room into the conservatory and quickly found the servants to prepare tea to help calm her nerves.

"I saw you listening to the inspector interviewing the neighbor. Then you suddenly ran to your carriage and disappeared. I asked him what had been said and that girl they call Flat Bitsy came up, telling us she had followed the cousin to a carriage. When she described it I knew immediately where you had gone. I also knew you'd walk unthinkingly into danger. I got here as quickly as I could only to find you standing with two obviously insane people who were pointing a loaded pistol at you as they bragged about their terrifying activities."

"I was a fool. I never thought Bradley would do anything to harm me. Bloody hell, I didn't even think he was involved until I arrived. What will happen to them? When the citizens discover who is responsible for these killings...I can't even imagine the backlash that will occur."

"Sheffield won't recover. The knife split open his intestines and I'm afraid his death will be slow and painful. I don't know about the woman, I'll leave that to Swanson and ultimately the Home Office, I suppose."

"I don't think Morgana's involvement in this matter is going to be something they wish to reveal. It's possible the world may never know these killings have been solved. There are places she can be sent. Perhaps Bedlam. It would be a fitting place for her and they'll watch her closely until the end of her days. Even if she tells them everything that has happened, they'll never believe what she may decide to say about her...accomplishments. But whatever they do I'm sure she'll never walk the streets freely again."

She drew his jacket closer around her and leaned back into the chair. The tension in her shoulders began to ease. "So you were right. Bradley was responsible. I don't understand why I didn't feel how deeply he'd descended into the darkness."

"Rowena, you have the ability, a gift, of understanding people. I told you before, every time you suspected someone had a dark side to their nature, I was able to confirm you were correct. But you were blinded by the years you had known Sheffield. The time you spent together as children. My love, your heart is too pure to see how depraved he'd become as he descended into the world of darkness."

"But..."

He held his finger to her lips. "You knew Bradley Sheffield was immoral, your imagination would never have permitted you to conjure visions of what such immorality meant."

She smiled for the first time since she'd rushed to the last and most chilling sight of murder by the killer they called Jack the Ripper. "But, you called me my love. Is this a sweet endearment or do you mean it?"

In answer, he drew her toward him

Lee Leslie

in a hungry embrace, and swept her into a
world filled only with passion.

———

CHAPTER THIRTY-ONE
October 1889

Percy, Bradford, Grace, and Fiona studied the small collection of newspaper articles. "It's a shame we didn't get recognition for our success. They only wrote stories about the deaths of Rose Mylett and Alice McKenzie. Most think it was the Ripper. It's sad so many of those we've been practicing on have gone totally unnoticed."

"Do you think Bradley figured out what we'd done?" Percy asked as he caressed Fiona.

"Why? He and that whore had no idea we followed them, saw what they did in Oxford. It was a great bit of fun pretending we were so upset when Emma Smith died. I'm just sorry we weren't able to watch them during their last game. It must have been quite exciting killing those five women. If it hadn't been for the nosey doctor I'm sure they would have gotten away with it." Bradford watched Percy closely. He liked how he took care of his little sister.

"So, do you have your bags packed? I guess you'll be sailing on Monday. It's a shame we won't have one last chance to have a bit of fun before we go." Fiona stuck out her lip in an exaggerated pout.

"The same question could be asked of you." Grace laughed. "You're leaving the day before we do. I hope you enjoy India, but if not you can join us in America."

"It's going to be strange, finding our fun without you two," Percy said, as he collected Fiona's cape and they prepared to leave. "We'll have to be sure to keep in touch. Perhaps we should devise a method of collecting points. When we get back together in a few years it will be exciting to see how many victims you've claimed and compare them to ours."

"Well the hardest part of the trip is

having to curb our appetites while we're on the ship," Bradford admitted as they walked their guest to the door. "You may have opportunities to practice along the way, so we won't keep any points until we are both settled in."

As Percy and Fiona's carriage pulled away, Bradford whispered in Grace's ear. "We won't be able to have any real fun on the ship. Maybe we should take a few hours and entertain ourselves tonight. I have that lovely set of surgical tools I ordered from Germany."

Grace pulled him toward her and gave his a passionate kiss. "Oh yes my love, let's."

———

www.ingramcontent.com/pod-product-compliance
Lightning Source LLC
Chambersburg PA
CBHW062006170626
46813CB00001B/57